D0108357

—

# DANZA!

# DANZA!

## Lynn Hall

CHARLES SCRIBNER'S SONS
NEW YORK

Library of Congress Cataloging in Publication Data
Hall, Lynn.    Danza!
Summary: While in the United States with one of
his grandfather's Paso Fino stallions, a Puerto Rican
teenager discovers his true feelings about horses.
[1. Paso fino horse—Fiction.   2. Horses—
Fiction]   I. Title.
PZ7.H1458Dan        [Fic]        81–8992
ISBN 0–684–17158–9        AACR2

3  5  7  9  11  13  15  17  19   F/C   20  18  16  14  12  10  8  6  4  2

Printed in the United States of America

This is a work of fiction. Any resemblance to
actual persons or events is purely coincidental.

# One

A sunrise breeze winnowed the grasses, silvered them and exposed the yellow and scarlet wildflowers scattered among them. In the distance, below and beyond the meadow, the Caribbean Sea softened away into the sky. The forest, green on black, rimmed the meadow on three sides and left only the southwest slope open to the distant view.

As though cued by the touch of the sunrise breeze and the golden light that came with it, two figures emerged from the forest on opposite sides of the meadow and progressed slowly toward each other, the boy dawdling in his enjoyment of the moment, and the mare distracted every few steps by one more swatch of grass that had to be eaten.

Their meeting was inevitable; there was no need to hurry to it.

The boy was eleven but small. He was a whip of bamboo clad in old pale jeans and a berry-stained blue shirt; he was huge dark eyes and unruly hair and silences that might have puzzled his family, had they noticed. Paulo Camacho was the second of six and the grandson of Diego Mendez.

The mare also belonged to Diego Mendez. Her designation on the farm records and on her registration was "Number Twenty," palomino mare by Ciervo out of Number Six, foaled April 12, 1951. If the pedigree was valid, her breeding was better than that of the other mares on Diego's farm, and Paulo chose to believe that it was.

"Hi, Twenty. How are you feeling this morning? No baby yet, huh?"

They came together, and the mare rubbed her head hard against Paulo's chest, easing the itch of a fly-bite near her eye. Her hide was a rich copper gold, dappled over her hips and flanks. Her cream-white tail swept, huge and full, to the ground, and her mane was twice as long as the depth of her neck. The forelock that Paulo's fingers straightened and smoothed covered the length of her head. In it, and in the mane and tail, were bits of greenery gathered in the forest as she brushed off her flies against the undergrowth.

Paulo bent low and looked up under the mare. Her udder was stretched and hard and hot under his palm when he touched it. A few drops of milk came, and the mare's ears flattened for an instant at the discomfort of his touch.

"Pretty soon now." Away from his grandfather, Paulo could make his voice sound as though he knew what he was talking about, and the mare accepted his authority.

"Just an easy ride this morning, okay?" He looked into her near-side eye for permission, decided that he saw it there, and led the mare, by a handful of mane, toward his mounting rock. Twenty was only fourteen hands tall, no more than average for a Puerto Rican-bred Paso Fino, and during the previous summer Paulo had learned to jump on her from flat ground. But now her barrel was distended with the bulk of her foal and Paulo didn't want to be bouncing and kicking against the unborn baby in his attempts to get above the curve of Twenty's sides.

He mounted instead from the rock, after a quick look back toward the house to be sure no one had followed. To be seen riding the mare, and to be tattled on to Grandfather and face the old man's derision—no, that was a higher price than Paulo wanted to pay, even for the fun of riding Twenty.

As Paulo settled onto the ridge of Twenty's spine the mare lifted her head and tail and moved forward, her eyes on the meadow before her, but her senses all tuned to the boy on her back, to the shift of his negligible weight, the touch of his ankle bones on the skin just back of her elbows and the pull of his hand in her mane. A pleasant lightness filled the mare, as it always did when Paulo rode her. It was this for which she had been bred, she and a hundred generations of her ancestors bred on this tiny island since Columbus brought the first horses to this part of the world. Just a handful of them at first, proud Andalusians and elegant Barbs and the small beautiful Spanish Jennets with their incredibly smooth four-beat gait. It was these horses and their descendants that had enabled the Spanish to conquer the New World, and when that work was done the horses remained, and in the relative isolation of this island they had evolved into a breed known as the Paso Fino, for the fineness, the smoothness of their paces.

As other breeds were developed to fulfill a need, pulling heavy loads or working cattle or jumping the stone fences of the English countryside, the Paso Fino was bred to give his rider pleasure. The uniquely smooth four-beat gait was retained and improved until it became the smoothest riding of all equine gaits. Beauty and elegance of carriage were prized and retained also, but no breeder sacrificed the cherished purity of gait for details of physical beauty.

Through the generations, the horsemen of Puerto Rico had come to feel the staccato beat of their horses' footfalls in the rhythm of their own heartbeats. The horses had grown to know a sense of completeness only when they carried riders to lift them into that beat, to move with them and balance their heads against their reins, to set the arch of neck and collect the hindquarters so that the movement was perfect and the perfection was as joyful to horse as to rider.

But for the mares this joy was rare. They were female. A man was less than a man if his mount was less than a stallion, and a mare's value lay in the fame of her sire, or her sons.

And so Paulo Camacho glanced again over his shoulder as he settled into Twenty's stride. Sometimes when he rode her Paulo pretended that she was Bonanza or Bravo or one of the other young stallions in their pens near the house. But a stubborn honesty in him made him dislike the pretense. It wasn't fair to Twenty. And Paulo knew, even if no one else did, that Twenty was the best of his grandfather's horses, mare or no mare.

His ankle bones touched her satin sides. There was

4

an unaccustomed hesitation before she responded. Although her unshod hooves moved noiselessly on the cushions of grass, Paulo could feel her footfalls in a gentle vibration through his seat and up his spine and into his heart. Smoothly as a sailboat in benign waters the mare bore Paulo across the curve of the meadow, her tangled two-foot-long mane wafting around him to brush back his unbuttoned shirt and tickle his stomach.

He giggled. The mare flicked an ear back toward him, and slowed her pace. He touched her sides again with his heels. Momentarily she surged forward, but slowed again almost at once.

"Don't feel like going fast this morning? We'll take it easy. You maybe don't feel too good, carrying that big old foal around inside you, huh?"

As they crested the hill, the other mares appeared, four of them with foals already at their sides, two with bulging bellies and one with neither foal nor expectation. That was Seven, a dark brown mare, bald-faced and blue-eyed and aged beyond use as a brood mare. Paulo looked away from her, knowing that her failure to produce a foal this year meant that she would be sold on the kill market.

Beyond the grazing mares a pole fence marked the boundary of the pasture, and the farm. Paulo managed to take down the top pole without dismounting, and ride Twenty over the bottom pole, but in the end he had to dismount anyway, to replace the upper pole. Sighing, he hauled Twenty by her mane toward a stump and climbed up onto her again.

She was reluctant to leave her pasture.

"Come on, why are you so lazy this morning? Just a

little ride, okay? Just up to our place and back, and you can go slow."

By hauling on her mane and leaning dangerously far to the right he managed to turn her and get her started along the track that led into the forest. It had been a logging road once, but was shrunk now to a narrow black-green tunnel into which the sunlight penetrated only in narrow spears that highlighted the flame orange blossoms of the flamboyán trees, the passionflowers, the scarlet and yellow and purple of the parrots and the smaller birds who stitched in and out of sight among the trees. There were satinwoods and mahoganies, survivors of the timber industry, Spanish elm and cedar and candletrees and here and there an old ironwood. Paulo lifted his head and flared his nostrils to the dank, perfumed forest air.

The mare stopped. Paulo urged her on with voice and heels, and she resumed the easy swing of her fino gait. A light sweat was coming under her mane and in her flanks.

The track, which had been rising steadily, crested and dropped and became a footpath too steep for logging trucks ever to have traveled. The mare picked her way down, easing her bulk sideways on the steepest parts.

At the bottom of the slope lay a valley choked with vines and splashed with wildflowers. To Paulo's left a waterfall came down at him, three stories tall but narrow as the span of Paulo's arms. It sheeted and splintered over and around rocks as big as cars and poured itself into a fern-rimmed pool that reflected black and scarlet and green from the forest that overhung it.

6

For a moment the horse and boy stood broadside to the waterfall and savored the rain of cool water that blew over them. Then, at the prodding of Paulo's heels, Twenty moved on again. She splashed through the stream below the pond, stopping to lower her head for a sip. Up the gentler slope of the far bank they climbed, the mare hanging her head for ballast on the climb, and Paulo aimlessly stripping leaves from the trees they passed.

Again the mare stopped.

"Just a little farther. To our place. You can rest there before we start home." He drummed her sides with his heels and she walked on.

The hair at the base of Twenty's ears began to ridge up in sweaty rims. Paulo saw it and looked down at the mare. Her whole body was wet now, and in Paulo's thighs he could feel a tremor in her body.

*It's coming,* he thought. *I'm going to see it get born.* The tremor was in him now. He exulted in the knowledge that he and Twenty would be going through the ultimate adventure together.

He dropped to the ground in a sudden surge of tenderness toward the mare, and led the way along the almost invisible path. The mare followed closely, her breath in his hair.

The path emerged in a broad clearing, an oval of brilliant emerald grass too flat, too symmetrical to be natural. Rimming the oval, like teeth around a jaw, stood tablets of stone taller than the mare. Carved on the faces of the stones were ancient gods smiling, scowling, dancing, or glowering omnipotent threats.

As he always did, Paulo stopped at the edge of the

oval and stood there with his arm across Twenty's neck, sensing ancient presences.

It was almost five hundred years since the Borinquén Indians had played their deadly games on this ceremonial ball court, games in which the gods, accepting their sacrificial tributes, were the ultimate winners. Five hundred years since the Borinquéns first saw the terrifying figures, half-man, half-horse, that had landed on their island from unimaginable worlds beyond the seas, and galloped and shouted and sometimes separated into two halves—men like themselves and the strange animals that shrilled and pawed the ground.

The Borinquéns were gone now, killed by epidemics that the invaders brought, or by slave labor in the invaders' mines. The ancient paving of the ball court had drifted over with leaves, and the leaves had turned to earth, and grasses and flowers and seedling trees had taken root there. Stone tablets had fallen and their god figures lay face down on the ground in the universal humbling of time.

The ball court was just an oval clearing in the forest now, a safe place for a boy and a mare to have early morning rides away from the ridicule of brothers and grandfather. The old gods were dead long ago, and Paulo felt no fear of them. But sometimes when the wind was just right, or when the sunlight caught a stone-carved face and gave it expression, sometimes when Paulo hit a beautiful solid cracking home run at Pony League practice, then there was a feeling in the back of his mind, almost a stirring of memory that reached far beyond his eleven-year life span.

But this morning Paulo's thoughts were all for the

mare. He paused not so much to feel the atmosphere of the place as to look at it from the viewpoint of a mare about to foal. Where would be the best place? If he were Twenty, where would he . . .

With a light shove Twenty walked past Paulo and into the circle of sunlight. Paulo followed. Through the sunny center of the clearing she ambled, and into the black shade beyond. There, near the rim of the ancient court, was a three-sided shelter formed on one side by standing stones and on the two flanking sides by stones that had fallen and become supports for wild tangles of trumpet vines. Here the mare felt sheltered.

Twenty stopped within the natural foaling stall and stood, head low. The painful shifts and pressures within her ceased to make her uneasy. She was in a good place for her delivery. There were no threats here. There was only the boy, but he was insignificant in comparison to the job ahead of her. She no longer had to carry him nor to respond to his heels; he could be ignored while she did her real work.

Paulo tried to follow Twenty into the small green square, but stopped when the mare glared at him. He backed off a few steps and made himself a seat on the corner of the fallen stone.

The mare's coat was chocolate brown now with her sweat. She grunted and swung her head around to bite at her flanks. She turned and stirred up the long grasses with her feet, and pawed to soften the earth beneath her. She lay down, rose again, and continued her turning, pacing, flank biting.

Paulo stared at her, his huge dark eyes following every move she made. Sometimes a shiver of uneasiness ran through him when she snapped at her flanks. Was she okay, he wondered? Should he have left her in the pasture? Should he be trying to get her back home or was it too late?

But then Twenty relaxed, and Paulo relaxed, too, and looked around at this place he loved, and thought how perfect it was that Twenty had chosen this time and place and was allowing him to be there. He remembered something his grandfather had said once. "Pablo, I'll tell you something about horses," Diego had said. "They are the only animal I know of that can choose when they'll drop their young. They can hold off going into labor until they want to start it, and that usually means when the humans have left them alone. They want privacy, even the gentlest pet horses."

Paulo felt the honor of the tribute Twenty was paying him.

Twenty jerked her head up and stared, wild-eyed, as amniotic water streamed down her hind legs. Paulo sat up, tensed for action. But nothing more happened, and Twenty relaxed again.

Paulo stretched out on his side, among the trumpet vines that cushioned the slab of rock. Their bright orange flowers brushed his elbow and his face. Staring at Twenty, Paulo's eyes went out of focus and he remembered the beginning of their friendship.

It was five years ago. The horses had just arrived—six mares and a stallion trucked up from Ponce one hot July afternoon. Those seven horses were Diego's dream; Paulo had not been too young to feel the impact of his grandfather's emotions as the horses clattered down the ramp. For as long as Paulo could remember, Diego had talked about horses, horses he had owned or known or ridden in the past, horses he wanted to breed. But there had been no money to buy horses. Diego had had only seasonal work in the sugar cane fields and the cane crops weren't good, this high up the mountains. There had been road construction jobs sometimes, and truck driving for the sugar central when Diego's back went bad and he could no longer do the grueling field work at cane harvest. There had been pigs and chickens and the garden to feed the family, but no extra money for buying fine horses.

Then suddenly it had come. A four-acre piece of land on Phosphorescent Bay near La Parguera, a tiny farm Diego had inherited from his mother, was sold to a rich American company for a tourist hotel. The price they paid for the land wasn't big, but it was enough to buy one fine stallion and a handful of comparatively inexpensive brood mares.

The mares were examined when they arrived, and gloated over and even petted by the children. But Diego's love was all for the stallion. Paulo stood aside and watched, and wondered at the intensity of his grandfather's absorption with the stallion.

Bonanza was magnificent, Paulo had to admit. He was a dark mahogany bay like fine old polished wood. He had two low white stockings on his hind feet, just to his pasterns, and a round white star on his forehead, which was usually hidden beneath the fall of forelock that covered his face. His mane hung to his elbow, and his tail was a full proud plume that brushed the ground even when he lifted it in excitement. His head was

11

small and fine and straight-planed, his tiny muzzle dominated by flaring nostrils.

Even in the somewhat dilapidated farmyard, against a backdrop of tin-roofed sheds and bamboo-fenced corrals, Bonanaza carried himself with tightly tucked head and arched neck, his clean fine legs moving in a quick-rhythmed dance.

The mares were turned out in their new pasture, and Bonanza was saddled. Paulo watched from a little distance while Diego pulled himself, somewhat stiffly, up onto Bonanza's back. They moved away through the dust of the farmyard, Bonanza snorting and shying at the rooster, at the sow squealing in her pen, at the younger children darting and yelling. But the old man sat erect, his thick body balanced over the horse's center of gravity, his white hair moving slightly around his ears. His square face was oddly blank, not from absence of emotion but from excess. As Bonanza turned and came back past Paulo, the boy was startled to see tears shining in Diego's eyes. Paulo looked away.

For several minutes the proud old man and the gleaming stallion circled the yard. Then finally they came to a standstill near Res. Res was nine, three years older than Paulo and superior in every way that counted. He was utterly fearless. He would walk in with the sow and her baby pigs, and taunt Paulo for staying on the fence. He was a better ball player, and he had curly hair and the kind of twinkly-eyed face that made older people say silly things about what a charmer he was going to be when he got older.

Diego dismounted and motioned to Res. The boy came forward, grinning, and stepped up into the stirrup with a boost in the seat from Diego. "Take him around," the old man said. "See what it feels like to be a man."

Bonanza bore his small rider away across the glaring expanse of dust. His hooves pattered their quick-beat rhythm as he carried his small rider in a smooth flow above the ground. Res grinned, and something in Paulo went sour.

The rooster ignored the approach of the horse until Bonanza was on top of him, then with a squawk and a great beating of wings he rose under Bonanza's belly. The horse, startled, half-reared and wheeled. Paulo's heart leaped, but Res laughed, regained his shaken balance, and sent Bonanza in pursuit of the fleeing rooster.

When Res brought the horse back Diego turned to Paulo. "Ride?"

Paulo hung back. He would have done almost anything to make his grandfather look at him with the same kind of pride that Res could engender on that big square face. Almost anything, but the horse was so huge, up close, so snorty, so nervous and quick in his movements.

Res said, "Come on, baby. You can ride up behind me. I'll steer him. All you have to do is hang on."

"But what if you fall off?" Paulo demanded. Res and Grandfather laughed, but then Grandfather started showing Res how to hold the reins in his hands, and they forgot about Paulo.

Paulo slipped around the corner of the house and started running, around the new corrals and out into the meadow where he could be alone. He hated Res for being better than he was, and he hated Diego for witnessing his failure and expecting no better from little baby Paulo. He even almost hated Bonanza.

But there were the mares. He walked out among them and felt better, seeing that they were as timid with him as he had been with Bonanza. They needed his reassurance that he wouldn't hurt them, and he needed to feel that something in this world respected him enough to fear him a little.

Most of the mares gently avoided him, allowing him to come within a few feet and then moving away a step at a time, grazing as they went. But one of them didn't evade him.

She was the copper-colored one with the long white mane and tail and the huge soft dark eyes. When Paulo reached toward her face she stood still and half-closed her eyes as though that small brown hand felt good against her face bones. As long as he was touching her, the mare stood still. If he removed his hand she shifted and reached for a bite of grass, but at his touch, on her leg or her ribs or down her tail, she stood still again.

Her back was up there above Paulo's head. It was as high as Bonanza's but it seemed a friendly back. A safe place to sit on. Maybe even a fun place.

When the mare's grazing took her near an outcropping of rock Paulo climbed up, sucked in his breath in a quick prayer, and flung himself across her back. She lifted her head but didn't move away. By the time he had thrashed and twisted and gotten himself astride, the mare was grazing again, twitching her skin against

14

the flies and lashing her long tail around and over Paulo's legs.

"I can ride, too," the boy cried silently. "See, Grandfather, I can ride, too."

He leaned down and wrapped his arms around the mare's neck, and bawled.

Twenty lowered herself to the grass, grunting. Paulo tensed, but held himself still. This was no time to distract her with reminders of his presence.

She lifted her tail and stretched her legs taut against the force inside her. She felt herself breaking open. Her muscles surged in a mighty squeeze.

A bubble of fluid ballooned out beneath her tail and within it were two hooves, one slightly ahead of the other. Another mighty contraction forced the bubble farther out. Cradled along the forelegs was a head, its outline just suggested to Paulo, through the membrane and the fluid that surrounded it.

For several minutes the mare rested and breathed and gathered her strength. Then came a tremendous contraction and the bulky mass of the foal's shoulders emerged.

Paulo's ears were ringing and he felt suddenly dizzy.

Twenty grunted and pushed, and the foal shot out onto the grass, where it lay wet and covered with the clinging birth sac. The sac was ruptured now, and the fluid that had cushioned and fed the foal for eleven months was drained away into the ground where, centuries ago, the blood of sacrificial offerings had soaked away to nourish the roots of the flowers.

The foal stirred and lifted its head in a wobbly gesture. A foreleg stirred and braced against the earth, but then relaxed for a gathering of strength.

After a few minutes Twenty shifted and scrambled to her feet, tearing the cord that still connected her to her foal. She turned and began to nuzzle and lick the baby. Its head weaved and wobbled under her shoving muzzle, and after a while it tried to struggle to its feet. It got halfway up, almost far enough for Paulo to see whether it was a filly or a stud colt. Then it sank again for another rest.

"Be a stud colt," Paulo breathed. Until that moment he hadn't cared much whether it was a stud or a filly, but now that he had witnessed the birth—something that he had never done before—Paulo felt a bursting kinship with this foal. It was as though Twenty was giving him this foal of hers, as though she knew that Paulo was big enough and a good enough rider that he no longer needed to ride mares in the privacy of the forest. He was ready for a stallion now.

Paulo knew, too, that if it was a filly it would be sold to the first buyer who came along after weaning time. But a stud colt out of Twenty, that would be a horse Grandfather would value. Bravo was a son of Twenty and Bonanza, and Bravo was a source of shining pride to Diego. If this one was a stud colt he wouldn't be sold. And he would be Paulo's special horse, as Bravo was Res's.

Paulo sucked in his breath as the foal made one more thrashing attempt to rise, and succeeded. It stood weaving atop its outpropped legs. Paulo slid down from his stone and approached. The foal felt damp and woolly under his palm. He lifted its tail and looked.

Stud colt!

He grinned till his face ached, and wrapped his arms around the foal's neck. It leaned against him for an instant, until Twenty pushed Paulo's arm away with her muzzle.

Paulo backed away then and watched while the foal shuffled and bumped toward the mare's udder. As his coat dried he became an odd shade of brown, almost maroon. His legs were a dull gray-cream, his mane and tail black. There was no white on him anywhere.

Through the long morning hours and into the afternoon Paulo waited and watched. He felt the pull of people at home wondering where he was, and Saturday chores piling up. But this was more important.

Finally Twenty seemed rested enough for the walk home, and the foal was maneuvering his legs reasonably well. Paulo took the mare by the mane and began the slow walk back across the clearing, down the hill, and across the stream.

The foal followed well enough until they came to the stream. Twenty whickered for him to follow, and he tried, but he couldn't lift his feet high enough off the ground to negotiate the slight drop into the water.

Paulo tried to wrap his arms around the foal and lift him, but the colt was too heavy. Paulo got behind and pushed, and with a squeal and a splash the foal was in the water. It came only halfway to his knees. He made a scrambling lunge and came out the other side and pressed close to the mare for reassurance.

Up the far slope they moved, and onto the old timber road. Paulo followed behind, now that Twenty was heading for home and needed no encouragement.

On the flat open track the mare increased her speed. Suddenly the foal lifted himself from his shuffling walk and swung into the beautiful rhythmic gait that is the birthright of every Paso Fino foal.

*Like a Spanish dancer,* Paulo thought. From his memory of Grandfather's list of names for future foals, Paulo focused on one name.

Danza.

# *Two*

Paulo lifted his face to the rain, closed his eyes, and smiled. They were big drops and they washed the sweat and dust from his skin. Beneath him, Twenty shook her mane, then paused and shook her whole body. Paulo hunched forward and laughed and grabbed her mane for balance.

Beside Paulo's left foot, Danza's tail lashed and sent raindrops arcing up over Paulo. The foal was three months old now. Already his mane was lying heavily to the right, and his tail reached a full inch below his knobby hocks. His head and neck and upper legs were sleek red, but his body still retained the maroon-brown wool in which he had been born. On his lower legs the black of his bay-stockings was beginning to show through the cream-gray hairs.

Paulo rested his foot on Danza's rump and felt the ticka-ticka motion of the foal's gait through the sole of his tennis shoe. Almost like riding him. Paulo shivered. Two more years to wait. An impossibly long time.

Time.

"Oh, boy," he said to the horses. "We better start back. Father's probably here by now and they'll all be waiting for me. I wish I could stay home this afternoon with you. Sometimes I get tired of watching Res win ball games. I'd like him a lot better if he'd strike out sometimes."

They were on a cane field road, a grassy track that separated the field from a neighboring grove of mangos. Paulo loved to ride in sugar cane. When he squinted at it a certain way and made his eyes go out of focus the towering spears of cane became clumps of grass and he and the horses became insects. Ants. A giant foot could appear over the cane and mash them to death.

He loved the tingle of safe scares.

But now there was a not-so-safe scare to think about: Grandfather's anger if Paulo made them all late for the ball game. Paulo's ankles touched Twenty's girth and the mare, headed for her home pasture, responded by extending herself in a ground-eating largo. With no break in her four-beat rhythm she reached out with her head and neck and lengthened her stride. Smooth as the wind she sailed across the grass, Danza galloping to keep up. Paulo leaned slightly forward into the rain-filled air, his eyes half-closed, a smile plastered onto his face like the wet hair on his forehead.

Of her own accord Twenty stopped at the fence that bordered her pasture and waited while Paulo dropped to the ground, let down a bar, and replaced it behind the mare and foal. But when he reached to remount her, Twenty shook her mane and evaded him. She danced away a few yards and lowered herself to the grass for a roll. Danza followed. It seemed to Paulo that the two of them were laughing at him, taunting him for his humanness.

The rain slacked away to an occasional breeze-blown spray.

Twenty lay upside down in the grass, her body doing a serpentine of pleasure, her hooves flailing the air. Back and forth she rolled, pushing first one shoulder and then the other into the soft wet earth. At last she rolled over and paused, gathering herself for the lurch to her feet.

In three running strides Paulo was astride her. She came up under him as he was landing. This time when she shook herself Paulo nearly lost his balance, the shake was so long and so vigorous.

Paulo rode across the pasture as near the house as he could without being seen. Then he slipped down, hugged Twenty, hugged Danza, and set out at a run across the smaller home pasture where the three yearling fillies grazed.

His father's massive, low-slung old Buick was parked in front of the house. The two men were seated on the porch, Ramon Camacho in his city slacks and his father-in-law, Diego Mendez, square and rock-faced and white-haired and looking all of a piece in his faded denim.

The house behind them might have been designed to match Diego. It was square and two-storied, its white paint weathered almost to nonexistence. The windows were glassless, as they had always been, their wooden shutters closed now against the rain. At one time the Mendez land had included almost a hundred acres of cane fields and valuable hardwood timber, with small citrus groves along the flanks of the mountains. The

21

house had been built during a time of prosperity and was bigger than most in the area.

But the prosperity was gone now. It had gone to America with Diego's five sons. One by one they had gone, to Miami, to New York, to California, gone where the big money was. With no one to work the land and no money to hire workers, Diego began to sell a field here, a grove there, until the farm had shrunk to thirty acres and Diego had shrunk to a joyless, caustic old man.

Paulo approached the porch.

"Son," Ramon said.

Paulo looked at his father and made a nodding motion with his head. He never knew what to say to his father.

Diego threw back his head and roared, "Fidelina, the boy's back. Lunch."

From within the house Paulo could hear his mother directing Mira through the table setting.

"Where have you been, Paul?" Ramon asked. He was a narrow-faced, handsome man, but some quality in him made Paulo nervous. It was as though the man were making polite conversation with a stranger because it was expected of him. Only with the younger children did Ramon relax and open his arms. Roberto came toddling out now. Paulo turned away from the sight of his father picking up the baby, holding him in that natural, affectionate way. He burned with the shame of his desire to crawl, like the baby, onto his father's lap.

"Out with the horses," he said in a small voice.

Diego scowled down from his height on the porch chair.

"Riding that mare again."

Paulo reddened and looked down. No point in denying he'd been riding, not with dirty, horse-hairy jeans like these.

"What mare?" Ramon asked, as he covered the baby's hand with his own to protect his eyes from Roberto's fingers.

"Twenty," Paulo muttered.

"Doesn't matter what mare," Diego spat. "Eleven-year-old boy with all those stallions to choose from," he waved toward the roofed pens where the stallions stood, "doesn't need to be riding any mare."

"But she's good, Grandfather. She's as smooth as any of the stallions and she's twice as willing, and you should see her largo. She never gallops in the pasture, and she can go faster in largo than the other mares galloping full out."

Diego needed no words to express his contempt.

The door opened and Mira called, "Lunch is ready. Hurry up or we'll be late for the game."

"Hurry up or we'll be late for the game," Paulo taunted. He had no real reason for picking on Mira, but he needed to, so he did. She made a face.

In the kitchen, with the family assembled at the table, Mira got her vengeance.

"Paulo's been riding Twenty again. Look at his jeans. Got yellow horsehair all over them."

"How do you know I wasn't riding Bravo? His hair's the same color."

"Cause you weren't, that's why."

"Be quiet and eat," Fidelina ordered. "We've got to get Res to his game."

Paulo lowered his head to eat, but looked at the rest of them under his eyebrows. There sat Res, all perfect in his white and black uniform, eating away with no sign of nervousness in spite of his game an hour from now. And why should he be nervous? He was the best player on the team, and one of the best in Pony League, and he never put out a bad performance. Paulo was good, too. In fact, he had a better eye for an approaching ball than Res did, but Paulo had nerves and he couldn't always control them.

And there sat Mira, only nine and she was already riding Bonanza and Bravo, and even Conquistador, the two-year-old stud colt who was so full of himself that Res couldn't always handle him. Neither could Mira, but she didn't let that stop her, and her nerve was an almost unforgivable quality in Paulo's eyes.

And there sat Manny and Lola and Roberto, too young to be any good for anything, and yet all of them got hugged and held when Father came home.

Paulo was the stranger here. He didn't belong with the rest of them. With Twenty and Danza maybe, but not with these people.

"I don't want to go to the game," he said suddenly.

They all looked at him.

"You can't stay home alone," his mother said.

"Why not? I'm old enough. You'll be back by supper time." Now that the idea had occurred to him, Paulo wanted very much to be alone this afternoon. Just him and the horses.

"Let him stay home if he wants," Diego said.

Paulo turned and studied Diego's face, trying to read whether Diego wanted Paulo to have his afternoon at home alone, as he wanted, or whether the old man just didn't want Paulo along on the trip to Maricao.

Diego went on. "You stay home and get the horses bathed for the show tomorrow. We're taking Bonanza and Bravo and the little black yearling. Think you can handle that?"

Diego's eyes were two black dots of challenge set deep in the leathery face. They stared into Paulo.

Paulo raised his head. "Sure. I'll take care of it. Bonanza, Bravo, and the yearling."

Paulo's mother sent a frown from Paulo to Diego. "I'm not sure I want him washing those stallions when there's no one here to help him if he gets in trouble."

But her father's eyes had the same silencing effect on her as they did on Paulo. "You want him to be a man? Then he's got to be able to handle those stallions. Or you want him to be a mare-rider all his life?"

The subject was closed. After lunch came the Saturday ritual of Ramon laying a stack of twenty-dollar bills on the table beside Diego's plate and Diego picking them up in a deliberate way, straightening the stack but not counting, then folding the money away in his shirt pocket. It was the family's share of Ramon's paycheck from Ponce Petrochemical. It paid for Diego's assumption of the family responsibility that should have been Ramon's; it paid for the freedom that Ramon needed.

Within a surprisingly short time, or so it seemed to

Paulo, the rest of them were folded away in the Buick and gone down the road toward Maricao and the ball game. With mixed emotions Paulo began to gather the garden hose and buckets and horse-washing towels. He was glad to be rid of the family; he ached at missing the ball game; he was eager to communicate with the stallions without Diego watching to see how he handled them. And he was just a bit nervous. Bonanza did rear sometimes when the water hit him, and it was possible for a person to get knocked in the face by a hoof, or stepped on. Trampled even.

He turned on the hose faucet at the side of the house and went to get Bravo. Start with the easiest first.

Bravo, at three, was a more settled horse than Bonanza ever would be. He was a buckskin, a son of Twenty and Bonanza. His hide was richly dappled gold turning black on his legs, muzzle, and ear rims. His tail was black but his mane, though mostly black, was overlayed with bright white above his withers. He had not yet been used for breeding, so his stallion-urges were still partly dormant, and because Res had worked with him every day of his life he was accustomed to boys' voices and movements.

The horse stood placidly tied to the banana tree in the side yard while Paulo played the hose over him, then lathered him and worked the suds into his mane and tail. Bravo closed his eyes and turned his head toward the spray and gave every evidence of enjoying it.

"Enough for you," Paulo said. He led the dark dripping buckskin back to his pen and left him tied there to prevent his lying down and rolling while he was still wet.

There were six pens under the tin-roofed structure, a

double row of three with an aisle down the middle. The walls of the building were nothing more than the bamboo fencing of the pens. In these pens, each about twelve feet square, the stallions lived their days, too confined ever to learn to gallop and risk jeopardizing the purity of their fino gait.

Four were in residence now: the herd sire Bonanza, the heir apparent Bravo, Conquistador who had been black last year but was turning blue roan this year, and the yearling colt Mirlo.

As he stood in the center of the aisle wavering between getting Mirlo over with and getting Bonanza over with, Paulo was struck by the realization that in another month or so Danza would be imprisoned here. For the rest of his life. He sucked in his breath at the pain of the thought, although it had never occurred to him to feel sorry for any of the other stallions so confined.

It would be Danza, he was sure. Of this year's crop of foals there was only one other stud colt, an unattractive dun-colored youngster who was simply no match for Danza's stylishness. And he trotted. It wasn't unusual for the young foals to trot from time to time in the pasture, but the little dun seemed to prefer a trot and almost never gaited with the correct four-beat Paso gait.

Paulo shook himself from his thoughts and opened Bonanza's gate. It had occurred to him that Twenty might enjoy a bath, and if he got the stallions done in time . . .

Bonanza snorted and tucked his head in the excitement of being led out.

"Settle down now, you're not going for a mare, only a bath." Paulo jerked on the halter rope and the stallion subsided somewhat, but still managed to swing sideways down the aisle as though the back half of him couldn't stand the slow pace of the front half. His feet pattered on the hard-packed earth in the flutter rhythm that was almost painfully exciting to Paulo.

As they emerged in the brilliant sun Bonanza stopped, startled.

A man stood watching them. Behind him was a car bearing the insignia of the U.S. Navy. Paulo stood still and let the man approach. He was tall, slim, military in his bearing although he wore slacks and a knit shirt with a tiny alligator on the pocket. The length of his face was accentuated by a receding hairline. It was a freckled, boyish face but the eyes were hard. They belied the freckles.

"That's a lot of horse you've got there, young man."

"I can handle him." Paulo said in English. He felt defensive and foolish.

"I'm sure you can. I was just admiring him, was all. I'm looking for," he glanced at a slip of paper in his hand, "a Mr. Diego Mendez. Is he here?"

Paulo shook his head. Bonanza began to swing sideways, impatient at the delay in whatever action was at hand.

"He went to a ball game this afternoon. My brother's playing. He's my grandfather."

The man rolled his eyes upward. "Ball game. I should have known. What else would a Puerto Rican be doing on a Saturday afternoon?" His smile hit Paulo in the eyes and warmed the boy.

"Might go to a horse show," he said pertly, "but we usually do that on Sundays."

28

The man laughed aloud then, and offered his hand. Paulo let go of Bonanza's rope with one hand just long enough to shake, then returned his grip to where it was needed most.

"I'm Major Kessler, stationed over at Roosevelt Roads. I'm retiring in a few months and going back to the States and I'm interested in taking back a few horses with me. Like to start breeding them up there. I was told that your grandfather had some good animals, thought I'd stop out and see if he might be interested in selling me a few. What's your name?"

Paulo's back straightened. "Paulo Camacho. I could show you the horses."

"All right, sir, you're on."

They started with Bonanza. Paulo led the gleaming mahogany stallion in a broad circle between the pens and the house. Bonanza tucked his chin, lifted his tail, and danced his quick-step through the dust.

When they came full circle Major Kessler said, "Do you think I could try him out?"

Paulo shook his head. "Grandfather doesn't let anybody ride him except the family. I could show you how he looks under saddle, though."

Quickly, before he could think about it, Paulo got out the saddle and bridle. Under the eyes of this admiring stranger Paulo moved with unaccustomed sureness as he buckled the girth and exchanged halter for bridle.

He pulled in a long breath, tightened the girth one more hole, and mounted.

The difference between this horse's power and Twenty's easy stride was startling. Bonanza's neck arched so tightly that Paulo had to gather in his reins, and gather them again in order to feel the touch of the horse's mouth. Through the form-fitting leather of the English saddle came tremors of power, up through Paulo's legs. Hard muscles bunched, and Bonanza moved forward, tossing his mane, playing metallic tunes with his teeth against the bit.

Paulo sat motionless. His hands were lost in the flow of mane, his legs rigid around the powerful barrel. He twitched his little finger against the rein and Bonanza veered right. Another twitch and he veered left.

It came to Paulo suddenly that Bonanza's show of barely controlled power was just that. A show. The flaring nostrils, the chin tucked almost to his chest, the sideways dance in Bonanza's gait were all for show. For fun. Because it was what the men who rode him wanted from him, and what the horse gloried in giving.

Was it a secret that everybody had known except him? Grandfather and Res and everybody? Well, no more. Paulo Camacho might be a little way behind, but he wasn't out of the game. Grinning, he circled the yard again, this time lifting the horse with his hands, pushing him up with his legs as he had heard Grandfather telling Res to do. There was a subtle change in Bonanza's footfalls as he settled into a steady collected fino rhythm.

"I don't suppose this horse would be for sale," the major said as Paulo slipped to the ground.

"No. He's our herd sire. Mirlo might be. I'm not sure. I'll show him to you. He's just a yearling."

The man seemed to be in no hurry, so Paulo got out

each of the stallions and put them through their paces. When he was through he said, "Grandfather's got some yearling fillies that are for sale."

They walked out to the small pasture and looked at the fillies, then climbed the fence into the brood mare pasture for a look at the foals.

Twenty and Danza were grazing near the fence. The foal's front legs were spraddled far out to the sides in his effort to reach the grass, so that he appeared to be bowing in homage to an invisible deity. The mare's head jerked up. She stared at the two figures, discerned Paulo, and began walking slowly toward him. The other mares moved away over the crest of the hill with their satellite babies beside them.

"Lovely mare," the major said, extending his hand toward Twenty's muzzle.

Paulo stared up at the man, and a glowing delight spread through him.

"She's my favorite. I ride her." Paulo waited for the man's reaction. He had never before admitted riding a mare, much less admitted it to a man, a powerful commanding major. He suspended breathing, and he hoped.

Major Kessler smiled down at Paulo. "Do you think your grandfather would mind if I tried her out, then? I've had so few chances to ride Paso Finos, and it's an experience."

He wanted to ride Twenty! He wanted to. All the time Paulo was running back for the saddle and bridle, and tacking up the mare, that thought sang through his head. If the major wasn't ashamed to ride a mare, then maybe it wasn't such a bad thing. Maybe in America it was all right. Maybe there was something Grandfather was wrong about.

Paulo watched in a semi-daze while the major mounted the golden mare and guided her out across the pasture, feeling out her mouth and her responses, feeling the gliding cadence of her gait.

Danza followed his dam, but not closely. He frisked along at her side or in front of her, leaping sideways from time to time and tearing away at a dead gallop, to circle back, gaiting, his small head and tail aloft.

As he rode, the major looked more and more often at the mottled red and brown foal. At length he dismounted and handed Twenty back to Paulo.

"How about the colt?" Major Kessler nodded toward Danza. "Is he for sale?"

Paulo shook his head. "He's a good one. My grandfather would never sell him. He might sell you some fillies or one of the older mares, I don't know. Maybe even Mirlo. But I'm pretty sure he wouldn't sell Danza. But you could wait till he gets home and ask him."

The major consulted his watch. "I have to be back at the base in an hour or so."

"There's a horse show at Maricao tomorrow. We'll all be there. You could come to that if you want, and talk to my grandfather then."

"Yes, well, I might just do that. Thank you, young man." He offered Paulo his hand. "I appreciate the time you've taken, showing me your horses, and I especially appreciate the opportunity to ride your fine mare. I expect I'll see you tomorrow, then." He strode away, leaving Paulo to strip off Twenty's saddle and bridle and lug them back to the shed.

Paulo sat on the porch steps. His back was turned to his father and grandfather, but there was an easy feeling among the three of them. The ball game had gone well, and the day's work was done. In the almost-darkness they watched Res maneuver the pickup truck toward the loading chute. He wasn't old enough to drive on the road, but Diego allowed him to practice in the farmyard. From the house behind them came the glow of kitchen light and the sounds of Fidelina and Mira packing the food for tomorrow's horse show trip.

"Ko-*kee*, ko-*kee*." A million tiny coqui frogs sang their twilight chorus in every field and forest on the island.

Paulo felt light, relaxed. Good. His grandfather had been unable to find any fault with the way Paulo had taken care of things. All three horses were bathed and brushed and polished, and Bonanza's two-foot fall of mane lay in shining waves that attested to a full half-hour of damp brushing after his bath.

Even more important, Diego had confirmed Paulo's intense hope that Danza was not for sale.

Paulo listened to the men's voices behind him.

Diego was saying, "I need to see him against other yearlings. I don't believe he has the substance he should for his age. I don't want a horse too fine-boned."

"He's elegant, though," Ramon said in an easy, sleepy way.

"Oh, Mirlo's going to be a beautiful animal. And

he'd bring a good price, as black as he is. But I think the little Danza will mature into a better horse."

Paulo said, "Will you sell Mirlo to the major if he wants him?"

Diego's voice took on a metallic edge. "I said I might sell the colt. I didn't say I'd let an American have him."

Neither Ramon nor Paulo dared to jar the peace of the evening by arguing that their business was selling horses and American money spent as well as any other.

# Three

On a morning in August Diego and Paulo brought
Danza in for weaning.

It was just after seven, but already the air was hot
and close as Diego led Twenty toward the stallion
pens. Paulo followed, staying as close to the colt as he
could. His stomach fluttered in dread and his mind was
full of the picture of Ebano, the fiery black colt who,
last year, fought the weaning process with such fury
that he broke both of his forelegs and had to be shot.

Twenty followed Diego quietly into the corner stallion pen and stood, resigned, while Danza skittered
away from the pen's gate two, three times before following his dam inside.

"You hold him now," Diego ordered.

Paulo's heart thudded as he approached the colt and
maneuvered to block Danza's view of the mare. He
wrapped his arms around Danza's neck and murmured, "Easy now, easy now."

Diego and Twenty were out of the pen. Res and
Manny swung the gate shut and secured it just as
Danza reared and knocked Paulo to the ground with

his flailing forelegs. The colt raced back and forth along the pen wall, sending shrill, piteous calls to the mare, who was his only security.

"You got a bloody nose," Manny announced as Paulo picked himself up from the dust.

"It's okay." Paulo's eyes never left the colt. He wiped the red smear off his face with the back of his hand and walked carefully toward Danza.

"Easy, fellow," he said over and over, in what he hoped was a soothing tone. Danza ignored him.

The colt reared and flung himself at the pen wall. Paulo sucked in his breath but released it when Danza's legs descended to the ground unbroken.

"How come he's getting weaned and not the rest of the colts?" Manny piped. He was six and had begun demanding explanations for everything that caught his attention.

Paulo ignored him. Res said, "Because Grandfather wants to take Danza to some shows in a few months, and the colts always get a little skinny after they've been weaned, so we have to give him time to get his weight back. And me and Paulo have to teach him to go in the long lines and you can't teach a colt much while it's still with its mother. See?"

Manny dropped from his perch on the fence and ran away. He wasn't interested in the colt or the weaning, only in the fun of asking questions and getting answers.

Res left to begin the morning work of feeding, cleaning, and exercising Bonanza, Conquistador, Bravo, and the yearling Mirlo.

"I'll do Mirlo and Conquistador," Paulo called. But Res waved him away.

36

"That's okay. You better stay with Danza for a while so he don't hurt himself."

Paulo took his eyes away from Danza long enough to see Twenty fighting against Diego's hold on her halter rope. They made slow progress across the near pasture to the mare pasture. Every few steps Twenty balked or swung in a circle around Diego. Occasionally she half-reared, straining her head back toward Danza and answering the pleading in his voice with pitiful cries of her own.

Fidelina appeared and stood with her arms folded along the top rail of the pen fence, her chin resting on her knuckles. Her face was long and thin, homely by some standards but a face in which sympathy and humor were never far from the surface.

"How is the battle going, Paulie?"

"Okay so far. He's a smart colt, Mama. I don't think he'll hurt himself like Ebano did."

"No. He's got you for a friend. That should help him through it. What's that, blood on your face?"

"I guess he banged me in the nose. It doesn't hurt."

She resisted the temptation to mother him. *They all have to be weaned,* she thought grimly, and left to continue her search for Roberto.

All that day, except for necessary absences, Paulo stayed with the colt and tried to soothe away the animal's terror with his voice. And as the day progressed and Danza grew tired of flinging herself at the pole wall, the colt began to notice the boy's voice, to lean into it for the reassurance that should have come from his dam's low whicker.

Paulo stood beside the colt, his arm over the woolly

body, his fingertips moving in gentle circles against Danza's skin in an imitation of the comforting motion of a mare's lips. Together the two of them looked across the near pasture to the place where Twenty stood leaning against her fence. The mare was a tiny figure in the distance, but her outline was eloquent.

Paulo wanted to go to her. He wanted to give her the same reassurance that he gave to Danza. His hands and his voice could help her through this, he knew.

But Danza needed him, too.

Without conscious thought his allegiance was given to Danza.

By the next day Twenty was back with the other mares beyond the crest of the meadow. Occasionally she raised her head and answered the call from her distant offspring, but already the severing process was well underway in her mind. Her udder was painfully swollen and chafed from the movement of her legs. With each step a stream of milk arced out through the sunlight or ran in a sticky trickle down her leg. But she had been through this before and she understood that the pain would go away soon. Already next year's foal had been forming for three months within her, and she knew it was there.

For the rest of the summer vacation Paulo spent as much time as he could in Danza's pen. He had Pony League practice three afternoons a week, and games on Saturdays, and there were Res's games to watch, and there were his chores with the brood sow and the chickens, and helping his mother protect the plantain and chick-peas from a marauding mongoose.

But there were still several hours a day in which he was free to work with Danza, and to play with him. The colt lost weight for a few weeks, then regained it on his new diet of good hay and grain. The last of his foal fuzz shed away and left him a gleaming bright red. His lower legs were not yet the pure black they would become, but were a mottled chocolate brown. They were clean, straight legs, fine-boned but big through the joints, giving promise of future substance.

The colt no longer looked toward the mare pasture, nor called in that direction. He watched the house instead, and whickered at the sight of Paulo, or for that matter at the sight of anyone who might be bringing him food or company.

There was an understanding among the family that Danza was Paulo's special charge in the same way that Bravo, three years ago, had been Res's. Although Diego didn't say it in so many words, everyone including Paulo sensed that it was Danza's function to make a man of Paulo. Often when the boy and the bay colt were working in the dusty expanse between the house and the pen shed, Diego stood in massive silence, in the shade of the porch, and watched the pair with a heavy satisfaction in his expression, satisfaction that was not so much approval as absence of disapproval.

The boy was riding Bonanza now, from time to time, just brief rides around the farm buildings during the stallions' morning exercise time, while Res rode Bravo or Conquistador. The fact did not escape Diego's notice, nor did the fact that Paulo was no longer coming home from unexplained absences, with his inner legs lined with palomino hairs. Nothing was said, but the old man occasionally grunted around his cigar.

The first few weeks of Danza's training consisted of Paulo leading the colt on a halter rope around the farmyard, along the road, in and out of the pickup truck in which Danza would soon be traveling to horse shows.

At first the leading was a mixed success. To the colt Paulo became his dam and it was as natural to follow him as it would have been to follow Twenty. But there were moments of flaring rebellion at the constant restriction of Paulo's hold on his head. He could take not one step outside his pen without feeling that control against his nose and poll. When his will differed from Paulo's the colt reared in fast, abrupt movements, sometimes grazing Paulo's chest or arm with his hooves.

But gradually the rearing ceased and the colt grew accustomed to matching his stride with Paulo's and following the boy confidently.

There were other lessons. Every day Paulo picked up each of Danza's hooves and scraped them clean with the hoof pick. When the hooves grew too long Paulo held the colt's head while Diego worked over each hoof with nippers and rasp until they were shortened and correctly angled.

Every day Paulo brushed the colt and combed the lengthening mane and tail until Danza stood quietly even when the brush passed across his belly.

By October Danza was ready for long-line training. Diego left one morning to spend a week at a sugar central near La Parguera to help his brother, who owned the central, get the machinery ready for the harvest season.

"Let's see if we can get Danza going in the long lines while Grandfather's gone," Paulo said to Res that afternoon as they jumped from the ancient school bus and began the walk home.

"Okay with me," Res said, "but why now?"

Paulo shrugged and scuffed up clouds of dust. "I don't know. He makes me nervous, watching me all the time. Just like he's waiting for me to do something wrong, so he can prove how dumb I am."

"Aw, you're crazy. He doesn't seem like that to me."

"That's because you never do anything wrong," Paulo flared. "And besides, he likes you better than me. He always did."

"You're crazy as a cockroach, you know it?" Res shoved Paulo's arm, and took off running with Paulo close behind. They slowed and walked on together, heads bent toward the ground. The road passed through a stand of bamboo so tall that the giant stalks met over the road like a vaulted church roof. A light wind moved the trees so that their hard smooth surfaces rubbed against one another and caused a high mournful screeching sound, as though the trees cried in pain.

"I'm going to get away from here." Res spoke grimly.

"You are?"

"I sure am, little brother. The minute I'm old enough. I'm going to California." He said the name as though California were a distant star.

"Why do you want to do that? What's the matter with here?"

"Here! Here is for old people, Paulo. There's no

41

money to be made here, nothing to do here. Why do you think all five of our uncles went to the States? And don't think Papa wouldn't go, too, like a shot, if he didn't have us keeping him here."

"But I thought . . . I thought you were going to stay here and take over the horse breeding business when Grandfather gets too old. That's what he thinks, anyway. Don't you love the horses?"

"Oh, sure, they're okay. I love Bravo, I guess, but I don't want to waste my whole life on them. I want to make money, man. I want to be where the beautiful girls are, you know?"

Paulo snorted. "You're only fourteen. You're too young for girls."

Again the grimness tightened Res's voice. "I'm not going to be fourteen any longer than I can help."

They ran the rest of the way to the house, skinned off their school clothes in favor of holey jeans and bare tops, and went to the pens to tackle Danza's training.

The long lines were of leather, twelve feet long and ending in eighteen inches of chain. Paulo threaded one chain end through the ring on the left side of Danza's halter, then ran it under the colt's chin and snapped it to the right-side halter ring. Then he threaded the other line's chain through the right ring, ran it over the top of Danza's nose, and snapped it to the left-side halter ring. Then he handed the lines to Res.

"I'll lead, you drive from behind. He's more used to following me."

Res took the two lines and positioned himself behind the colt and a little to the left, while Paulo stood beside Danza's head and reassured the colt. Danza's ears alternately pricked and flattened at the unpleasant pressure of chain around his muzzle.

"Ready?" Paulo said.

"You bet. Let's go."

Paulo stepped out, leading Danza by the cheek strap of his halter. The colt moved forward willingly but stopped when he felt tension in the lines. Res clucked to him and Paulo urged him forward, so he moved out again.

This time Res exerted a light but firm pressure on the lines. Danza flattened his ears and snorted, and tucked his head toward his chest to avoid the chain across his nose. Immediately the cadence in his footfalls settled into a beautiful four-beat fino step.

"He's got it," Res shouted. The colt snorted and leaped aside and tangled himself in the lines. He tried to turn toward Paulo, and tangled himself further. He spun in a quick circle and gathered the lines around his legs as a fork gathers spaghetti in its tines.

Res began to laugh, and Paulo joined in. As the boys tried to unwind the lines, the colt continued to circle away from them until boys, colt, and lines were so hopelessly interwoven that Danza was forced to a standstill, and Res and Paulo tripped over each other and ended rolling and laughing in the dust.

When it was over they sorted themselves out and began again.

Diego Mendez slowed the truck and pulled off the road into a grassy track skirting a cane field. All the way up from La Parguera the trembling in his hands and arms had gathered momentum. Now, with home just over the next hill, he was forced to stop until his nerves were conquered.

He turned off the ignition and sat running his hands up and down, up and down around the curve of the steering wheel. He saw neither the hands nor the cane field beyond his windshield; his vision was filled by the bloody, mangled body of the man, nameless man, what was his name, Juan? Pedro, Pablo—what was it? It seemed unbearable that Diego had worked beside the man for four days, oiling and repairing the cane choppers, had seen the man fall to his death on the chopper's blades, like the teeth of a baracuda, and could not remember his name.

The name and the face became those of Paulo Mendez, Diego's eldest son. It was a cane-cutting machine, not a mill's choppers, that had shredded the life out of Paulo, but the horror was the same. For the last several years Diego had been able to sleep free from nightmares about Paulo's death, but now this morning's accident at the sugar central brought it back with sickening force.

"They must not see me like this," he vowed, "shaking like a foolish old *jibaro*. I must make it stop. Oh, my sons, why aren't you here? Why did I let America take you away from me? I need you here. Better to be safe in America than dead in a cane field like Paulo, you told me then. You wanted to go. You all wanted to go away from our home. And now the little ones. Res with his California talk. And Manny, who will follow Res in whatever he does. Only Paulo might be left to me. This Paulo, this little twig of a mare-rider, left in the place of my own Paulo. Oh, well, he's young. And he loves the horses. Maybe he'll stay—"

The ache of unshed tears rose in the old man's gullet, but he clenched them down. In a few minutes he was able to trust himself to turn the truck's key and kick it into life.

In the farmyard a triangle of figures moved. The apex of the triangle was a bright red colt moving with chin tucked and feet snapping with brio, in a clear ticka-ticka beat. The long lines fanned out behind and beside him, each line terminating at a sweaty, dust-crusted boy.

"Turn him around to the left," Paulo yelled. "No, swing out more. Swing out farther, or else he'll start backing up again and get over your line."

"You sure are getting bossy," Res retorted, but he took a few half-running steps as Danza pivoted around Paulo and started back toward the house.

"Here comes Grandfather," Res said suddenly. "He's back early. Wonder why."

"Got done, I guess. You're getting slack, dummy, take up your slack, he's going too far around. Straighten him out."

As the truck passed Paulo, he grinned at Diego. Danza was going surprisingly well after only four days in the long lines, and Paulo ached with eagerness to show him off to Diego.

The truck went by with no flicker of interest from its driver in the boys and the colt. Diego parked under the banana tree and stepped stiffly out.

"Come on," Paulo said, and together the boys urged Danza into a quick flowing fino step. The hooves were not lifted high; they just cleared the ground, but the brio was beautiful, the quick snapping motion at the pasterns. With an exuberant if unprofessional flourish they drew Danza to a halt in front of Diego.

Paulo opened his mouth to say, "Look how well Danza is doing," when his grandfather's expression froze him into silence.

"You damn little fool," Diego shouted. "Don't you have any better sense than to push that colt that fast? How many times have I warned you about that? You push for speed at his age and you're going to have him trotting. A fine animal ruined because you've got to show off."

Diego walked away into the house. White-faced, Paulo stared after him.

Suddenly he tossed his line to Res and mumbled, "Take him, will you?"

He started away at a walk, but beyond the stallion pens he broke into a wobbly run across the near pasture. He skinned through the fence and ran on.

She came toward him, exuding reassurance with every placid step. Grass hung from between her lips and her long tail waved away the flies without rancor. She stopped when Paulo reached her and flung his arms around her neck. His fists were a dragging weight against her mane and his nose pressed somewhat uncomfortably against her shoulder bone, but she stood patiently until he had fought down the threat of tears and lifted a dry, hardened face up to the sun.

# *Four*

The buildings around the plaza were strung with Christmas decorations. Bright silver balls festooned the small palm trees that edged the plaza. A manger scene with live animals stood in front of a church of ancient Spanish construction at one end of the plaza, while at the other end the statue of Ponce de Leon wore a wreath of Christmas greenery.

From the public television set came the sound of Christmas choral music, but only those sitting close to the set could hear. Trucks were pulling into the quiet little mountain village, pulling in and parking around the edge of the plaza, and disgorging whinnying, clattering horses.

Diego Mendez waved to a friend as he slowed the truck and parked it near the others. Beside him sat Res and Paulo, dressed like their grandfather in traditional horse show attire. They wore high black boots over white trousers, dark blue jackets, and white Panama hats.

Paulo's clothes had been Res's until he outgrew them, but their glory was undimmed, for Paulo. The clothes were more his than Res's, because Res had never genuinely cared about the horse shows. Res was good with the horses, as he was with everything, but Paulo knew his brother had never stood, dreamy-eyed, stroking the high black boots or hugging wrinkles into the blue jacket.

Paulo got out of the truck somewhat clumsily. The boots were still too big for him and were stuffed with rags in the toes; they didn't bend in the right place over Paulo's toes and he had to walk stiff-footed.

Ramon's Buick pulled in beside the truck and spilled out the rest of the family—Ramon and Fidelina, Mira, Manny, and the babies—and three neighbors who had come along to see Paulo's and Danza's first show.

With a businesslike hauteur that almost hid his trembling nerves, Paulo ignored parents and children and aligned himself with Diego and Res. The three horsemen wrestled down the truck's tailgate-ramp and led the three horses out.

Danza came out in a great leap that cleared the entire ramp. His eyes moved nervously about; his skin was wet with nerve-sweat. Bravo came sedately down with no show of tension, but Bonanza came in little snorting leaps, fired by the excitement that he knew was coming.

The three horses were tied to the truck's box, the near-black mahogany bay, the dappled gold buckskin with his brilliant black-and-white trim, and the small red-gold colt. The three horsemen in graduated sizes went to work with brushes and cloths, removing the travel dust from the horses' hides, polishing hooves, cleaning ears and faces and sheaths, while Manny and

48

Mira took buckets and ran to the plaza fountain for water for the horses to drink.

As he brushed Danza's mane Paulo watched Manny and Mira go for water. His old job. But he was almost twelve now, an exhibitor. Boots and jacket and everything. And of course his own horse to show. For a brief painful moment he wished himself back in the ranks of little-kid water carrier and watcher from the sidelines. So much could go wrong. Danza could panic and bolt through the crowd and Paulo not be able to hold him. He could kick or bite someone else's colt and get Grandfather into trouble. He could simply make such a poor showing that Grandfather would be openly disgusted with Danza and Paulo.

A flatbed truck had pulled up in front of Ponce de Leon. On the truckbed were the loudspeaker equipment and the tables for the show officials and the entry-takers. Diego went to make the entries. Paulo continued to brush Danza, hoping to steady his trembles with the rhythm of the brushing. Fidelina reached for Paulo from time to time, twitching his tie or brushing off his shoulder. Paulo gritted his teeth against his desire to hit her hand away.

The show ring began to take form, a more or less open space between the flatbed truck and the row of horse trucks, with a gathering crowd of watchers delineating the other two sides of the ring.

The bell in the church tower rang nine times.

Paulo felt suddenly sick.

The loudspeakers stuttered to life, and the announcer made his welcoming speech. Hats were removed and children shushed for the singing of the national anthem, and for a lengthy prayer from the village priest calling for sportsmanship and honesty among men to equal that of the horses.

The announcer said, "We will begin in five minutes with the Bella Forma classes, starting off with weanling colts. Have your weanlings ready."

Paulo was shaking so badly that Res had to exchange Danza's rope halter for the black leather show halter, and to attach the chains of the long lines.

"What are you so scared about?" Res said in his unfeeling tone. "All we have to do is drive him around a couple of times."

"Good luck," Fidelina and Ramon called in unison as the boys started away with Danza. Diego said nothing, but watched so casually that he seemed not to be watching at all.

There were four colts in the class. The first to enter the ring-space was a leggy black, a local colt and an obvious favorite of the crowd. The colt began his circuit of the ring with his two handlers in his wake. Midway around, he panicked and reared, and tried to bolt from the ring. The crowd cheered the colt for his display of spirit. The colt settled somewhat and continued around the ring to the judge, then around again in the reverse direction. The judge nodded and waved the colt to lineup position in the center of the ring, then motioned to Paulo and Res.

Quickly the boys dropped back from Danza's head to their positions just back of his hindquarters, and out to the side far enough for balance and control. Already

Danza's head was tucked against the pressure of the lines and he was in forward motion.

Ticka-ticka-ticka-ticka. His small hooves beat a flutter rhythm on the cobblestones. Paulo's eyes were glued to the colt's head for steering purposes, but his ears heard the quick, steady fino beat, and it ruffled his heart.

Danza shied only once, as he rounded a corner and saw his own reflected movement on the huge, high-mounted public television screen. But he settled back into his gait almost immediately and completed his round, and the reverse round, then went to join the black colt in the center lineup.

The crowd cheered with moderate enthusiasm, recognizing a fine colt and an excellent performance, but not wanting to diminish the chances for their local favorite.

The last two colts entered and made their rounds. Paulo, standing now beside Danza's head, barely saw the two performances, so relieved was he at having survived Danza's showing, and having done well. He did glance once toward the crowd. A man was looking at him, smiling into Paulo's eyes. A familiar face—who—oh, yes, the American major.

The announcer spoke, and Paulo forgot the major.

"In Weanling Bella Forma, first place goes to La Noche, owned by Federico Rameriz, shown by Federico and Juan Rameriz."

The crowd exploded in cheers and applause as the black colt's handler collected his ribbon and left the ring.

"Second Place to Danza, owned by Diego Mendez, shown by Paul and Orestes Camacho."

Again the crowded plaza rang with cheers. So long as he hadn't defeated their local colt, the villagers were more than willing to honor the fine bay.

Paulo nearly drove Danza over the judge in his excitement. He collected his ribbon and led Danza back to the truck, grinning so hard his cheeks ached.

Diego waited beside the truck, his face impassive. "He's a better colt than the black," was his only comment, but for once Paulo sensed no personal criticism in his grandfather's tone. When he handed Danza's ribbon to Diego, the old man shook his head and said, "You keep it."

Paulo had a startling urge to hug his grandfather. He turned away instead, and met the smile of the approaching major.

"Good job, Paulo." The man extended his hand and shook Paulo's. He didn't offer his hand to Diego because the old man was helping Res get Bravo ready for his class, but the two men nodded and the major smiled.

"Good morning, Mr. Mendez. Nice to see you again." The two had met with some frequency during the past few months at horse shows.

The yearling class was finished, and the two-year-olds were nearly done. Res and Diego began making their way through the crowd with Bravo between them.

"Come up here. We can see better," Paulo said to the major. He ran up into the truckbed and climbed to a perch atop the slatted side panel. Major Kessler stood beside him, arms along the top of the panel.

"Are you still looking for horses to buy?" Paulo asked.

The major sighed. "Well, more or less. I'll be retiring next month and going home. I'm going to start looking for a farm right away, and I will be seriously looking for breeding stock then. But in the meantime I'd sure like to get a good stallion lined up. That bay colt of yours is looking better all the time."

Paulo grinned. The combined glow of Danza's good showing and the major's respect was almost too much for him to hold, sitting still.

"He sure is. But my grandfather would never sell him to an American. He probably wouldn't sell him at all, since he's turning out better than Bravo."

Paulo and the major both kept their eyes on the distant figure of Diego.

"Why, Paulo? He said he'd sell me mares. Why won't he sell a stallion to an American? He nor any of the other breeders I've talked to."

Paulo shrugged. The reasons were too complex, too shaded for him to understand, much less to explain to this stranger. They had to do with manhood, with the five sons of Diego Mendez who were lost in the unreal distances of America.

Bravo, with Diego and Res in tow, sailed into the ring. Paulo shook his head. Bravo was too extended. His neck was straight instead of arched and no amount of half-halting from Diego's and Res's lines would get the horse sufficiently collected. Bravo was strung out in an easy corto gait, the same footfall pattern as the slower, showier fino, but without the brio-snap at the pasterns. It was a lovely easy corto that could have taken horse and rider for miles of effortless riding. But it was not a competitive show ring gait for Bella Forma class. Bravo ended fifth out of six.

Bravo was handed unceremoniously to Paulo, and Res and Diego went back into the ring for Bella Forma, Four Years and Older, with Bonanza.

Paulo said, "My grandfather's getting pretty mad at Bravo. Maybe he'd sell him to you."

"If the horse is bad enough he might sell him to an American, right?" The man's voice was tinged with frustration.

Paulo shrugged and turned his attention to the ring. Bonanza was the first stallion to enter and circle. He was black with sweat and the red linings of his nostrils were visible even to Paulo. Bonanza snorted with every step, but his movements were a study in controlled power. Diego and Res had only to keep their lines taut, and the horse did the rest.

He was an extremely short-bodied animal, fine-headed and slim-legged, with beautifully flowing curves over his neck and croup. All of his parts blended and balanced, and even his two-foot fall of mane failed to make him look front-heavy and unbalanced as in some Paso Fino stallions. He bore a strong resemblance to the medieval Spanish chargers pictured in Paulo's history books. He needed only an armored knight to complete the picture.

But his moment of glory was brief. Into the ring came the other stallions one by one, blacks and bays and chestnuts, a roan and a buckskin and a cremella. The crowd was compressed back upon itself to give the stallions more room.

Eventually there was barely enough room for the

horses to stand and no room at all for them to gait. A side street was cleared of traffic and the judge gaited the last four entries there.

Out of the seemingly hopeless melee the top contenders emerged, Bonanza and six others. In the final pronouncement Bonanza was placed third in the class of twenty-seven four-and-older stallions. Although Diego did not quite smile as he came out of the ring, there was a lightness to his expression. Paulo could tell he was pleased.

During the General Condition classes Diego and Res joined Paulo and Major Kessler in the truck box where they could see the ring over the heads of the people on the street. Diego was one of the old purists among Paso Fino breeders; he had only a casual interest in the General Condition classes, for horses who performed the relaxed, mid-speed corto form of the gait, and the more extended, high-speed largo form. For him, only the beautifully collected, slow-motion fino gait drummed its rhythm in his blood and only those horses who were born to this specialized gait were worthy of being exhibited.

Paulo looked down from his perch and waved at Manny, who, with Lola and the baby, were watching cartoons on the public television. Mira was out of sight, but Paulo knew she'd be somewhere near the center of the horse action.

His attention returned to the class in the ring. Six horses were in largo, circling the cramped area at top speed, their ears flattened, manes streaming. Like Twenty, Paulo thought. She can fino with the best of them, but she can corto and largo just as well as these horses, and there aren't very many Pasos who can do both kinds of gaits, at least not as well as she can. I wish we could show her.

He was startled when Major Kessler said, "Your little palomino mare ought to be in there."

Diego snorted, and Paulo said, "These are all stallions at this show. There are a few mare shows, in the fall, but we don't ever go to them. Not very many people do."

The major was silent. Danza, who was tied near the major's legs, reached through the slats and lipped at the man's trouser legs.

"I like this colt of yours," Major Kessler said casually.

Diego grunted and began unwrapping a cigar. He didn't offer Major Kessler one.

"Danza," the major said. "Nice name. What does it mean?"

"It's a dance," Paulo answered when it became obvious that Diego didn't intend to. "A sort of a formal, old-fashioned dance."

"I'd like to have him," the major said softly. His words were aimed out into the air. "You could name your price."

Diego dropped his match and ground it out savagely with his heel. Without a word he jumped down from the truck and began saddling Bonanza for the Fino Class.

Softly, so only Paulo could hear, Major Kessler said, "Does he hate my guts personally, do you know, or is he that way with all his prospective customers?"

Again Paulo felt a fire kindling inside him toward this man who seemed not to know that Paulo Camacho

56

was a no-account little kid. Under the man's side-long glance Paulo felt himself stretching and swelling. Maturing.

"Oh, he likes you okay. He just doesn't like Americans."

The major gave a short, bitter laugh.

"What I mean is, I don't know. He has awful strong feelings about his stallions and I just don't think he wants his bloodlines anyplace but here in Puerto Rico."

"But he'd sell me mares."

"Well, he has to sell some horses, to make a living. And he doesn't feel the same way about the mares. See, my grandfather's ancestors go straight back to the old Borinquén Indians who owned this island a long time before Columbus discovered it. And then he came and brought the first horses and they scared the daylights out of the Borinquéns because they thought the horses and riders were all one animal, and they thought the horses were gods. And then the Conquistadores came and took over the place and killed just about every-body except a few of the Borinquéns that got away and hid up in the caves in the mountains. And some of the Conquistadores' horses got away, too, and lived up there in the mountains with the Borinquéns and the horses and men really started loving each other. You know? So my grandfather's feelings about his horses go way back. Four hundred years. And I've got it in my blood, too." His voice rose to a note of pride.

The major nodded, but could find nothing to say, and a few minutes later he excused himself and disappeared into the crowd.

\*　　\*　　\*

In the months that followed, Paulo and Danza seemed almost competitive in their spurts of growth. The boy's face began to emerge from the soft curves of childhood and show the planes and angles that would be his through his mature years. His body was less like a whip than a supple young sapling. Daily riding, in the open now on the stallions, hardened his thighs and gave substance to his stringy arms.

In the colt, the maturing process was even more striking. As a yearling Danza's body lengthened, as did his head and neck. His mane hung a full foot in length and his tail was nearing the ground. His color was a rich bright red just gilded with a copper sheen.

He lived out his days in the pen beneath the rusting tin roof of the stallion shed. Mornings and evenings Paulo came for him and took him for exciting drives in the long lines. Sometimes they circled the yard, scattering chickens in a glorious flurry of squawks and feathers. Sometimes they went down the road, through the bamboo grove and out onto the main road.

Often on Sundays Danza joined Bonanza in the back of the truck and they went to try their luck at a local horse show. In Yearling Bella Forma Class, and then in Two Year Old, Danza more and more frequently came out of the ring with top honors.

Paulo outgrew his first set of handed-down horse show clothes and moved up to Res's more recently outgrown boots and jacket.

As Bravo showed more and more clearly his tendency to be a corto-largo horse rather than a fino specialist, he was sold to a family near Ponce, for their children's use. Res took the loss in so philosophical an attitude that Paulo knew there had been no strong love between his brother and the buckskin horse. Res was sixteen now, and spent as much time as possible learning to ride surfboards. Preparing for California, Paulo told himself.

After Bravo left Paulo began to ride Conquistador, the blue roan, almost every day. Conquistador was less dependable than Bravo or Bonanza, and Paulo was afraid of him. The horse tended to lunge forward as soon as Paulo's foot was in the stirrup, and more than once Paulo landed on the ground before he landed in the saddle. Once mounted, though, Conquistador became reasonably settled except for occasional shying. He was a tense horse, and easily startled.

Paulo dreaded his daily rides on Conquistador, but he knew that, behind an impassive face, Diego was watching him. Measuring him. Waiting for an opportunity to criticize Paulo's efforts with the horses. Paulo's feelings toward his grandfather simmered close to hate sometimes, and it was this heat in him that drove him to face Conquistador day after day.

And he must be good enough to ride Danza when the time came. He knew that he had to keep his balance honed and his muscles hardened for his real work in life.

Danza.

More than once Paulo had seen the marks of a rider's legs on Twenty's back, and corresponding sweat marks on Mira's legs. There were times when he ached for the old times, the good secret rides with Twenty in the stone-rimmed ceremonial court in the forest. But if Mira was riding the mare, then he could not. He wasn't sure what logic there was, if any, behind this knowledge of his, but he felt it too strongly to question it.

One morning at breakfast Diego said to Paulo, "Well? When are you going to ride your colt?"

Paulo stopped cutting his pineapple slice.

"Is he strong enough to carry me now?"

Diego snorted. "No more than you weigh? Sure."

He tried to eat a few more bites of breakfast, but his hands shook and his stomach knotted against the food. After a few minutes Fidelina caught his eye and motioned toward the door with her head.

Paulo bolted for the door.

*This is it. It starts today,* he sang inside himself. Fear was there, too, but mostly glory. For the past two years and two months, since the moment of Danza's emergence onto the grass in his wet wrapping, not one day had gone by without Paulo's hands on the bay colt, his voice in Danza's ears. They knew each other, the two of them, and there was a bond there.

The colt waited, his head over the pen gate. He was nearing his full height now, a little over fourteen hands, and his body was broadened and lengthened. As yet his neck was somewhat thin and straight, but the stallion muscling was beginning there.

It took Paulo longer than usual to exchange Danza's rope halter for the tighter-fitting show halter in which he had his long-line workout. His fingers seemed unable to cope with buckles. Twice Paulo glanced over his shoulder toward the house. Diego was nowhere in sight.

Good.

Instead of the long lines, Paulo snapped shorter ropes to the halter on either side, and led Danza out into the glaring sun.

The horse felt the tremble in Paulo's touch and smelled a disturbing taint in the boy's sweat. He moved sideways uneasily, alert for whatever it was that was frightening Paulo.

"Whoa now. Easy."

Paulo waited until Danza was standing quietly. Then he moved to the horse's side and made a jump. Danza sidestepped nervously.

Paulo led him to the truck and positioned him near the rear fender. This was a familiar place. Danza had often been tied to the truck at horse shows. The horse relaxed.

With two easy steps Paulo mounted first the fender then the horse. As his legs settled around Danza's girth Paulo was washed by a feeling of completeness, as though his other half was now rejoined to him.

Danza threw up his head and stiffened.

"It's only me, only me," Paulo chanted softly and stroked the satin neck.

Danza danced sideways. The weight on his back shifted only the slightest bit, then balanced itself. The boy's voice was in his ears; the boy's hand was on his neck.

Danza stood, taking in the strangeness.

Danza felt a lifting in the lines, heard the soft clucking sound that meant he was to move forward.

His feet did a patter dance in the dust. This was all right, then. The voice and the touch on the lines as he had always known them. All that was different was the weight of Paulo on his back and the feeling of needing to balance himself under that weight.

Gradually the colt relaxed and tucked his chin and hindquarters, as he did when he assumed his fino gait in the long lines. As always, the rhythm of his own motion brought up an ancient joy in the horse, but today it was augmented by a feeling of partnership with the boy, a feeling he had missed without knowing that he missed it.

They moved together as dancers move, raising dust and chickens and glory.

Neither the colt nor the old man who watched from behind the kitchen shutter saw the tears of trembling emotion that streaked the dust on Paulo's face.

# *Five*

The spray from the water hose made a rainbow against the morning sun. It was not yet eight o'clock but already the day was steaming with a damp, oppressive heat.

Danza stood quietly under the spray, head low, ears relaxed. Down his glistening sides and legs the residue of the shampoo's foam retreated and disappeared. Paulo wadded the long, thick tail and dunked it in a bucket of rinse water, then swished it through the air with a wringing motion that flung drops over the boy, the banana tree, and Roberto, who stood watching.

The baby was a sturdy boy of four now, with the look of Diego in his square little face. To Paulo, who had been waiting in vain for another spurt of his own growth, it seemed that Roberto was catching up to him with dismaying speed.

Paulo stood back and surveyed Danza. Nothing disappointing about his growth, for sure. Danza was a three-year-old now, and a fine eyeful. His body was short-coupled, as was Bonanza's, but round-barreled. The full curve of his stallion neck continued in one fluid line over smooth withers, brief back, and roundly sloping croup. His legs were straight, clean planes, as was his head. Beneath the forelock that covered its length, Danza's head was a pure, straight profile, broad between the eyes but tapering to an unusually fine muzzle.

His mane, dripping water now, hung nearly to his elbow, a rippling sheet of blue-black against the copper red of his hide.

Mira came running from the direction of the mare pasture. Her arms were piled to her chin with long-stemmed wildflowers that fell and trailed after her, scarlet and gold and yellow, passionflowers and blooms from the forest's flamboyán trees.

She stopped near Danza, panted hard for a few minutes, then said, "I'll do his flowers. You better go change your clothes and get ready."

"What time does the parade start, again?" Paulo asked.

"Ten. I told you. Go on, I can do him."

Paulo glanced at the sun for a feeling of how late it was getting, then sighed and left Danza to her. She was better at getting the flowers to stay in his mane than Paulo was, and he knew it, but hated letting her do anything with Danza.

He was almost to the house when a car drove in. Paulo glanced at it, assuming it to be his father arriving for the weekend, but it was a strange car, one with the anonymity of a rental car. There were almost as many of them on the mountain roads as the *publico* taxis, and they usually carried American tourists out to see the less public beauty of back-roads Puerto Rico.

Paulo went toward the car, prepared to give a lost tourist directions. But it was not a stranger who emerged from the car.

The man approached smiling, his hand extended to Paulo as though he were greeting another man. "Remember me? Major Kessler. I was here two, three years ago looking at horses. You're not—"

"Paulo." The boy grinned and gave his hand over to the man's grip.

"No! You were just a boy the last time I saw you. Is your grandfather around?"

"He's here, but we're all getting ready to leave in a minute. This is our town's Saints' Day and I'm riding in the parade. And my brother's pitching this afternoon in his Babe Ruth game, so the whole family's going and they'll probably be in town all day."

The major's face lengthened. "Not a very good day to talk horses with him, then, is it?"

Paulo shook his head.

"Well, then, I won't bother him now. Tell you what, maybe I'll just go on into town and watch the festivities. I might be able to catch him later on. I have to be in Ponce tomorrow afternoon, though, and I did want to talk to Diego while I'm up this way."

"Looking for horses to buy?"

Major Kessler grinned. "Did you ever know me when I wasn't? But I've got my farm now, up in north Louisiana, and I've got to buy stock for it. I've been visiting a few breeders, picking up mares, but I'm still looking for a stallion."

"Can't find any good ones?" Paulo asked, half teasing. Already the good feelings were coming back, the feelings of stature and maturity this man engendered in Paulo.

"Oh, hell, this country is wall-to-wall good stallions," the major spat. "That's what's so damnably frustrating about the situation. You people have more good stallions than you know what to do with, and you just won't part with them. And up there, up home, we're crying for good breeding stock. Americans are just finding out about Paso Finos, and there's a tremendous demand for them, and without stallions . . ."

Paulo ached for the man. To want a good horse, to have the money to buy him, and yet not to be allowed to. Awful. Awful to think of not having Danza.

He said, "Could you take some of our mares and breed them to whatever kind of stallions you have in your country?"

Major Kessler shook his head. "You could, but you'd lose the paso gait. The gait is a recessive, genetically speaking. Do you know what that means?"

Paulo shook his head.

"It means, in practical terms, that as long as you breed two Paso Finos together, you'll always reproduce the gait, but that if you breed to a horse that isn't a Paso Fino, the offspring would only carry the gait as a hidden characteristic. They might reproduce it in the next generation, but that horse wouldn't likely have the gait itself."

It was too confusing for Paulo, and time was passing. "Well, I've got to get ready. I'll watch for you in town, and wave at you in the parade."

"Good talking to you, Paulo. And Paulo, would you put in a good word for me with your grandfather?"

Paulo smiled and shrugged, and ran for the house.

The truck was lightly loaded, for once. Only Danza rode in the back, and only Paulo and Diego in the cab, separated by a battered red ice chest that contained the family's lunches and Cokes. Bonanza was at home with a stiff, swollen hock, a gift from a mare who had objected to being bred. Res and the rest of the family were detouring to pick up one of his team members and would be following later in the Buick.

Paulo's arm rested on the ice chest; his fingers drummed the hollow metal until Diego frowned at the noise.

"You can kind of see his point," Paulo said. "He's trying to breed good horses and nobody will sell him a stallion. I feel kind of sorry for him."

"You want me to sell Danza to that gringo?" Diego flared.

"No, not Danza. I don't want you to sell him to anyone. Naturally. But we do have some nice colts, and it isn't always easy to find buyers for all of them. Everybody around here is raising their own colts, and lots of them are as good as ours. We could sell one to Major Kessler for lots more money than anyone around here would pay."

"Money! You think I put my heart and my sweat into these horses year after year just to make money? You got a coconut between your ears, Pablo. If we sell our good stallions to America, then—" He paused, searching for his argument.

"Then they might be able to breed Paso Finos as good as we can, you mean?"

"No. They could never do that. They don't have it in their blood, like we do for four hundred years."

"What, then, Grandfather? Why won't you sell him a colt?"

The leathery face seemed to close. All expression left the deepset eyes, and Paulo knew that logic had no place in this argument. But he thought about the frustration in Major Kessler's face, and he imagined the shining gratitude the man would pour down on him if Paulo could talk Diego into a sale. He made one more attempt.

"Don't we have any colts you might let him have? Not any?"

Diego was silent for so long Paulo was about to repeat the question. Then he said, in a voice softened slightly, "I might let him have Ratón."

"The Mouse? You'd sell him the Mouse? He may be a gringo, and he may be desperate for a stallion, but he's not crazy."

Paulo shook his head as he pictured the Mouse. For all of the colt's two years Paulo had watched the Mouse develop, expecting some improvement as the animal matured. If anything, the colt grew less attractive. He was the offspring of a mare Diego had bought already bred. Her owner assured Diego that the mare was in foal to the current Island Champion, but Diego had been unable to get written proof of the breeding. The mare herself was unimpressive and had only been bought for the foal she carried.

The Mouse was a muddy gray-brown color, which

seemed to be fading toward cremella this year. His head was large and Roman-nosed, his ears unpleasantly long, his tail set much too low, and his hind feet splayed outward so badly that his hocks knocked as he walked. And as if his physical shortcomings were sufficiently damning, he showed a marked tendency to trot in the pasture. He was not yet started in his training. Diego lived in hope that a buyer would come along and relieve him of the colt before any training time was wasted on him.

"Don't even offer Ratón to the major," Paulo said. "It would be an insult."

Diego remained impassive.

Danza's nerves stretched like piano wires strummed by the excitement of the parade. The band music clashed in his ears; flags and streamers startled his eyes, and in the far corner of his right-eye vision, flashes of scarlet and yellow bounced alarmingly close, the blossoms in his own mane. A passionflower tickled one ear.

There was a tremor in Paulo's thighs and in the hands that spoke to Danza's sensitive mouth. Without a steady Paulo to reassure him, the horse felt insecure. The village was familiar to him, and the crowds that lined the plaza were like the crowds at horse shows, but the band music, the increased sense of excitement in the air, and the flowers in his mane combined to create a need in the horse for a calm rider to lean into.

The band noise changed from the cacophony of tuning up to the familiar strains of the national anthem. Danza broke into a nervous sweat and, as Paulo's hands prevented him from going forward, he began to lift his feet in the rhythm of his fino-dance, marching in place just as the members of the marching band in front of him were doing, awaiting the signal to move forward.

For a tiny mountain village, the town had managed to draw an amazingly large crowd for their Saints' Day celebration. There were *santeros* peddling their carved figures of the saints, and *décima* singers, and gaily decorated booths selling caramel custard flan and coconut ice cream and tacos. Bookmakers wove through the crowds offering odds for the afternoon's cockfights.

Through his saddle flaps Paulo could feel the trembling hardness of Danza's muscles. Through the reins came the clack of teeth against bit as Danza snatched nervously at his restraint. His neck arched high in front of Paulo; his right rein was lost in the cascade of black mane and brilliant flowers.

From his height astride Danza Paulo could see across the crowd to Major Kessler, whose height gave him a half-head advantage over the people around him. The man looked neither at the band nor the vendors, nor the crowds that pressed close to him. He looked steadily at Paulo and Danza. Even from this distance Paulo could read longing in the man's face.

The band moved forward.

With the smallest relaxation of his little fingers, Paulo released Danza. Forward they glided, somewhat sideways as Danza asked for more speed than he was allowed. The forward movement seemed to steady the horse. Danza and Paulo together relaxed into the enjoyment of the moment. Paulo sat perfectly straight, perfectly motionless as Danza floated him over the cobblestones. Shifting only his eyes to the left, he met the major's gaze.

The man smiled, and the smile kindled such pride in Paulo that Danza felt it, and responded.

Paulo watched most of the afternoon ball game from the back of his horse. Since he had dropped out of league baseball two years ago, to avoid conflicts between horse show Sundays and ball game Sundays, his interest in the sport had begun to fade. It was fun to watch Res pitch, especially now that Paulo felt no need to be as good a ball player as his brother. But it was even more fun to sit stroking Danza's neck and feeling the admiration and envy of the horseless people around him.

Occasionally he dismounted and boosted up a small child or two, or even three, and led them in circles behind the bleachers.

As the game went into the ninth inning Paulo rode back into town in search of Diego and the truck. He found them near the cockpit, where the cocks were still savagely bloodying and killing one another to the cheers of the men who watched.

Diego was just emerging from the crowd. Major Kessler was leaning against the truck, apparently waiting in accordance with a prearranged agreement.

"I'll follow you out in my car," the major said as Diego climbed into the truck. Paulo led Danza up the ramp and began to unbridle him.

The truck coughed and died. Started, coughed, and died again. Diego ground the starter. Nothing.

Paulo sighed and replaced Danza's bridle. "I'll start

riding him home, Grandfather. If you get it started you can pick us up along the way, okay?"

Diego waved him away. "It's in the starter," he growled. "Been doing this all week."

As he rode out of the plaza toward home, Paulo looked back over his shoulder. Diego and the major were half lost under the hood of the truck.

Good, Paulo thought, smiling. If this was a storybook the major would magically get rid of all of that old truck's problems and Grandfather would be so grateful that he'd offer to sell him a good colt. That little black one, maybe. And the major and his colt would go back to America and live happily ever after.

America. Paulo tested himself, as he had begun to do from time to time, to see whether he had yet begun to itch for that country. Already, at fourteen, his friends were beginning to talk about getting away from home, going up to America to get rich in New York or Miami. And Paulo knew the hunger was strong in Res.

But Paulo felt none of it. With the village behind him he settled into his saddle and looked around, trying to see the familiar hills as if they were new to him. Winding road of blue crushed lime snaking between coffee groves, a distant hillside glowing with orange-blooming flamboyán trees; in the far distance over his left shoulder, the soft blue-white of the Mona Channel, and ahead the mountains forested with mahogany and satinwood and candletrees.

"I don't know much about America," he told Danza, "but without all this, and especially without any Paso Fino horses, I don't see how it can be much of a place."

Danza snatched at his bit and asked for more speed.

"I'm not supposed to let you. Grandfather says a fino horse should never be allowed to go faster than a fino. It might spoil your gait."

But the day was beautiful, and Danza still had a flower or two clinging in his mane, and Paulo was full of a lightness that was just short of excitement, residue from the parade and anticipation of being with the major this evening. And it was three miles home, three miles that would pass at no more than walking speed if Danza were held in fino.

Paulo gave the horse a fraction of rein and for the first time he felt Danza's flowing-water corto gait. Like Twenty's! He grinned in spite of his uneasiness at what Grandfather would say if he knew.

After a little Paulo's fingers gave another fraction and Danza stretched into a flying largo. Through his dazed enjoyment of the speed Paulo wondered at Danza's ability to perform these gaits when, since the fourth month of his life, he had been confined to a small pen and exercised only under restraint, only in his slow-motion fino gait.

The fields whirled past in a blur of dark green. Brilliantly colored birds rose from the roadsides. They passed a thatch-roofed farm shack beside a drying rack covered with coffee beans. Paulo half-closed his eyes and breathed in the fragrance as he passed.

At a crossroads stood a weathered box of a building, its tin roof rusted through. Paulo could remember when it had been a factory that made children's shoes and employed a dozen people.

He passed a hump of green beside the road, an old

car body grown over with a luxurious blanket of vines. It had been there for as long as he could remember.

A pair of stone pillars rose from among the giant blades of a cane field. They were all that remained of the once-impressive entrance to Sabaña Grande, at one time a vast sugar plantation.

Paulo slowed Danza and stared thoughtfully at the pillars. He had only a vague idea of what had happened to the big sugar plantations. Something about the invention of big machines to harvest the cane more cheaply than men could do it, only the machines didn't work out very well in the high mountain plantations, so the lowland cane growers had the advantage and could sell cheaper, and put the mountain plantations out of business. And it had something to do, too, with America finding cheaper places to buy sugar. Hawaii, if he remembered right from his teacher's explanation.

So now if anybody wanted to make any money they had to go to America to do it. Paulo felt a touch of his grandfather's resentment toward that country, where everything seemed to come so easily and everyone was rich.

He became aware that Danza was dripping sweat and the unmaned side of his neck was lathered white where the rein rubbed. Guiltily he pulled the horse down to his proper speed. At any moment Diego's truck might come roaring past and it would be big trouble for Paulo if the old man knew he'd had Danza in largo.

His thoughts resumed their direction. He stroked the heated neck and said, "Well, old horse, here's a couple of us that aren't going to go running off to America.

We'll stay right here and be partners, okay? You make the colts and I'll sell them, and Res can go to California and chase girls around the beach."

They were passing through the shady tunnel of the bamboo grove, almost home, when Diego's truck roared up behind them and passed, with the major's rented car close behind. Paulo allowed Danza to fino as fast as he dared. He ached with impatience to be home, to be with the men when Diego showed the major the colts.

To see which of the long-legged youngsters, if any, were offered, a good one or Ratón. Or only mares.

As he approached the house he could see the two men lifting the big red ice chest out of the truck's cab and setting it on the ground. Paulo smiled grimly. Something was going wrong with Diego's back, something no one was allowed to talk about, but which prevented Diego from riding as often as he used to, and from lifting without assistance things he had always lifted alone. Like the ice chest.

As Paulo rode up and dismounted, the major looked at him and smiled, and the smile included both Paulo and the horse. But Diego was already marching away toward the pasture gate. Major Kessler hurried to follow.

Swiftly Paulo pulled off Danza's saddle and bridle and hung them over the fence. Danza started toward the water trough but Paulo hauled him by the mane into his pen.

"You can have a drink after you cool off. I'll be back."

Diego and the major were some distance away by

75

now, across the near pasture. Paulo swung shut the gate to Danza's pen and flipped up the loop of rope that held it shut. Then he turned away and ran toward the men.

A good colt? Or Ratón?

The loop of rope fell across the edge of the gate's end pole, and there it lay, balanced nearly in place but holding nothing.

Danza's skin steamed. His muscles trembled with fatigue. The excitement of the parade, the long afternoon of standing and moving about in the glaring sun of the baseball field, then the long swift ride home, a delight of unaccustomed speed but a tremendous drain on muscles he seldom used, all of these combined to bring him to a point of near-total exhaustion.

And he was dry. His dryness was almost a pain in him. Nothing to drink since early morning, and he had sweated profusely for much of the day.

He paced around and around the small enclosure. He lifted his head over the top rail and tried to see Paulo, but the boy was out of sight.

He went to the gate through which Paulo should be bringing him water, and nudged it impatiently with his nose.

The gate creaked open.

For the first time since his confinement three years ago, Danza broke into a gallop just for the few strides from the pen to the water trough. It was a large trough straddled by the pasture fence, so that the stallions could be led out to it handily from one side, while the yearlings were free to drink from the other. But the water was low just now. No one had filled it since early morning.

Danza lowered his head and drank until the last, rust-flecked dregs came up through his mouth. Then he turned, shaking his mane, and started back toward his pen.

But he paused, turned, and followed another scent across the yard to the ice chest. Its ill-fitting lid was up a crack, just enough to release the smells inside. Cold water. Ice. Half-melted remains of a carton of coconut ice cream.

He pawed at the chest, and jumped back at the metallic clatter it made as it fell backward. He came close again and nosed at it. The lid opened far enough to admit his stiffened, probing upper lip. Then his muzzle. Then his whole head.

He sucked up the ice water. It numbed his neck going down. He picked up the sodden cardboard of the ice cream carton and nodded his head until the sugary-tasting stuff fell with a splat to the ground. When he'd licked up the last of it, Danza returned to the chest and gnawed and crunched at the ice within it.

His thirst relieved, the red stallion lowered himself to the dust for a luxurious thrashing roll, then scrambled to his feet.

He stood, swaying suddenly. An uneasiness was beginning in his belly. Head lowered, he moved back toward the security of his pen.

A short time later the pain began in earnest.

# Six

Paulo hurried through the evening feeding and watering of the stallions. The rest of the family was home by now, and supper was being laid on the picnic table in the side yard. In spite of his embarrassment at the scene in the pasture earlier, Paulo was eager to get back to the major, who had agreed to stay for supper.

Res appeared and began leading the horses, one by one, out to the trough.

"Danza's gate's open," he called as he passed it, leading Bonanza.

"Shut it, will you?" Paulo was loaded down with hay.

Res returned the mahogany horse to his pen and led Danza out. The horse moved slowly and refused to drink the fresh water that was running from the hose into the trough. Res's mind was full of the happy possibilities that Juana Valdez had seemed to be offering with her eyes as he came off of the ball field this afternoon; he didn't notice the tenderness with which Danza placed one foot before the other.

As Res led out the third horse he said, "What happened with the major this afternoon? Did Grandfather offer him a colt?"

78

Paulo snorted. "Ratón."

"Didn't buy him, did he?"

"Course not. He's not dumb." Paulo's flaring protectiveness of his major surprised even himself. "First he thought Grandfather was kidding. Then he got about half mad but he didn't say too much. Tried to talk Grandfather out of that little black colt. Ended up buying two mares, though."

He distributed armloads of hay to each of the pens.

"Which mares?" Res asked, not really caring.

At Danza's pen as he dumped in the hay Paulo turned toward his brother to answer. He didn't see Danza's pain-dulled eyes. "Seven and that pinto."

"She's nice. I'm surprised the old man let her go, especially to an Americano."

Paulo grunted as he picked up the grain buckets. "Yeah, she's a good mare; Grandfather just doesn't like pintos very much. The major really liked her, though. We showed him her colt from last year and he liked the colt, too."

Together the boys walked toward the house. The noise of the children racketing about the yard covered the single low groan that came from Danza's pen.

As the night deepened Danza's pain grew intolerable. The ice cold water striking the horse's overheated system sent shock waves into the farthest parts of his body. Fever followed, a searing internal heat that burned to the roots of his hair follicles.

In his hooves, the fever set up a swelling in the layer of tissue that joined the outer shell of his hooves to the inner bony core of his feet. The pressure grew unbear-

able as the inflamed tissue bore outward against un-
yielding hoof wall, inward against sensitive and un-
yielding bone.

Danza lay on his side, his legs stiffened with pain,
his eyes alternately closed and opened wild-wide. He
was terrified.

Although his hearing was excruciatingly heightened
by the fever so that he heard with pain every voice in
the house, Danza did not hear the one sound he
needed: the approach of the boy.

Paulo jumped down from the porch into bright
morning sun. After a few hours of porch-visiting last
night, and most of a bottle of stout island rum, Major
Kessler had decided to accept Fidelina's invitation to
the use of their couch for the night. After that the talk
settled in, in earnest, between the two men. Diego
hadn't noticed, and the major hadn't minded, Paulo's
silent presence and the boy had stayed in the shadows
of the porch until well after midnight, listening to the
horse talk.

He swung open Danza's gate and said, "Hey, wake
up, you lazy—

"Mother of God."

He didn't know that he screeched for help, but they
all came, the little children and Paulo's parents and
Diego and the major. Paulo stood frozen, staring at the
rigid, wild-eyed horse lying at his feet. He barely felt
the blow from Diego's elbow as the man knocked him
out of the way.

Voices lashed around him, Diego's fury and the
children's shrill excitement equally meaningless.

80

Only one word connected in Paulo's mind, and it grew to monstrous proportions.

Founder.

With stark clarity his mind saw Danza's gate swinging open last evening, saw the horse's listlessness, which he had mistaken for simple weariness, saw the ice chest lying open and empty in the yard, a sight that only faintly had registered in passing last evening.

He remembered shutting the gate just before he ran to catch up with Diego and the major, but he couldn't remember dropping the rope loop down over the post.

These thoughts went through Paulo's mind in a blur as he dropped to his knees beside the horse's head. Under his stroking palm the disk of Danza's jawbone felt unnaturally warm.

He barely heard the major's saddened good-byes, nor his saying he would be back in four or five weeks to pick up the mares he had bought.

A towel flung angrily struck Paulo's face. Diego stood beyond Danza, a water bucket in his hand.

"Soak that towel and start sponging his legs and feet."

"Will it help?" Paulo begged.

"Probably not. I expect he's a dead horse. But it might cool down the fever in his feet. Res, you keep bringing him water when he needs it. Cold as you can." And the old man stamped off.

Day after day Danza lived on. He lay limp and hopeless in his pen while Paulo sat beside him. The fever subsided but left a burned-out digestive and nervous system. Danza was too weak to stand, but even if he had had the strength, his feet would not have borne his

81

weight. There was too much residual pain from the swelling of the connective tissue between his hooves and the inner bones of his feet.

Every day the horse grew thinner and Paulo grew more desperate. He offered wisps of hay. He pulled fistfuls of tender pasture grass and held it to Danza's lips. He pressed handfuls of grain against Danza's teeth. If the horse accepted a mouthful and swallowed it after interminable chewing, Paulo's hopes soared. But more often than not the offerings were blown away by Danza's hopeless sighs.

Paulo was unable to hold Danza's head up in drinking position long enough for him to take in water, and Danza was too weak to support his own head, so Paulo squeezed water into Danza's mouth with a sponge.

One morning when Paulo began to bathe Danza's legs—a part of the routine that he had continued long after the fever was gone, in the hope that it might do some good or at least feel good to Danza—he was startled to see a path of bare skin where the sponge had rubbed.

He stared at the sponge. It was covered with red hairs, solidly covered.

Paulo reached out cautiously and stroked Danza's neck with his palm. Where he touched, the skin was left bare and Paulo's palm was coated with shed hair, its roots destroyed by the intense heat of the founder fever.

By the end of the day the horse had turned from bay to a ghastly shiny blue-gray of naked skin. The ground around him was drifted with red.

And yet Danza did not die.

A few days later Paulo grasped the long black tail to

move it aside so that he could clean the pitifully small amount of manure produced by Danza's almost non-existent diet.

The chunk of tail came away in his hands, a four-foot-long hank of coarse black hair.

Paulo flung himself down along Danza's back, his arm around the horse's neck, his face buried in the wealth of mane that fanned out on the ground. He cried, hoping desperately that Grandfather wouldn't see him, but unable to stop.

Why can't he just die and get it over with? His agony was wordless but the thought was strong in him. I killed Danza and he's the only thing in the world that loves me. That I love. And Grandfather knows I did it. All these years he's never liked me or trusted me, and he was right. How could I ever grow up to be a horse-man, his partner, if I could do something like this to a horse I love so much?

He shifted his knee and a swatch of mane, the last vestige of Danza's glory, pulled easily from the horse's crest.

And still Danza did not die.

It was late evening, all but dark. The coqui frogs raised their evening chorus across the island. "Ko-*kee,* ko-*kee.*" As Paulo left Danza's pen and started toward the house he could see the glow of Diego's cigar, head high to a sitting man, in the blackness of the porch. Through the window came the sounds and the blue-white glow of the television set that held the rest of the family indoors.

There was a tightening inside Paulo. He tried to

avoid Diego when he could. He found it impossible to meet the old man's heavy gaze.

But tonight avoidance was impossible. "Pablo."

Paulo stopped at the steps.

"Is he any better?"

Paulo looked away and muttered, "Don't think so."

"I'm going to have to shoot him, then."

Paulo gasped as though the blow had been physical.

"Four weeks now, and he keeps getting worse. He's in pain. I have to do it."

"But he wants to live! He's trying so hard. And I don't mind taking care of him. Let him try a little longer, please. Please."

Diego turned his head away and gazed stolidly out over the valleys. The conversation was over.

Aching with despair, Paulo went into the house.

As the door slammed behind him Diego allowed his throat muscles to relax. They hurt from the clenching of emotions. The magnificent horse wasted, dying out there. And the boy dying inside, too, from the guilt of it and the pain of losing his horse.

The pain of losing. Diego knew that pain. Losing a horse, a son. A wife. All the loving things. All the best of life. For his Paulo to die because of a misstep too near the machinery; for little Paulo to lose his stallion, his *amigo,* because of a gate loop; the towering unfairness of it sent waves of rage through the old man, rage against a God too weak or too heartless to prevent such things.

In the dark he crossed himself, fearful of his thoughts.

He backed away from them and returned to practical things.

I should have shot the horse when it first happened, he thought. But I hoped. Well, tomorrow then. No, not tomorrow. The major will be coming for his mares. After he goes.

When Paulo entered Danza's pen the next morning his ankle brushed against a front hoof grown long and deformed, lengthened and curled in upon itself like an elf shoe. At the touch, the hoof broke off and toppled to the ground.

Paulo stared, horrified.

Protruding from the bottom of the leg was a stump of tissue oozing blood and encasing the denuded inner bones of Danza's foot.

Paulo's ears rang and dizziness threatened to overcome him as he bent and picked up the empty hoof.

It's the end. Over and over the words sounded in his head. It's the end. Danza . . .

"Good God!"

The major's voice close behind him startled Paulo out of his threatening nausea.

"That's not Danza."

Paulo turned and looked helplessly at the man, the hoof still in his hands.

Major Kessler stepped inside the pen and looked more closely at the blue-gray pile of bones that lay at the toes of his glossy boots. "How long has he been this bad? What have you been doing for him? Does he eat anything at all?"

"Sometimes," Paulo whispered.

"What is your vet doing for him?"

"Vet?"

The man spun on Paulo. "Yes, vet. *Veterinario*. Haven't you had him looked at even?"

Wide-eyed, Paulo shook his head. "We never do. Grandfather takes care of them. Everyone does it that way. A *veterinario* would have to come from Ponce or somewhere. And they wouldn't be able to do any more than Grandfather has done."

The major's grimness softened for a moment as he looked at Paulo for the first time and saw the gray cast to his skin, the exhaustion and hopelessness in every line of the boy's body.

Then the major hardened. "Where is Diego?"

Before Paulo could answer, Major Kessler was striding across the yard toward Diego, who was just coming from breakfast.

"You're killing that horse," he said harshly.

Diego stiffened. "It's the founder that's killing him, not me."

"It's lack of medical care, Mendez. Give him to me. Let me see if I can save him."

"Why do you want a dead horse?"

"I might be able to save him. If I can get him back to the States, to the vets at the university, they might be able to pull him through. Otherwise he sure as hell is a dead horse."

Paulo looked from one man to the other. The power of the two combatants almost overshadowed the issue. Could there still be hope for Danza? Was America such a place that their *veterinarios* could do a miracle like that?

"Grandfather, please!"

Neither man noticed him.

Diego's eyes narrowed. "If you did save him, what then?"

"I'd have the stallion I need. I've been all over this island for the past four weeks and I've bought nine good mares, including yours." Major Kessler waved toward the stock truck that stood, unnoticed until now, across the dusty yard. "I've got my mares, but no one would sell me a stallion. Mendez, I am desperate, desperate enough to take a chance on a long shot like that." He waved again, this time toward the stallion pens where Danza lay drawing flies to his fresh-blooded stump of a foot.

"No!" Diego shouted. "You took my sons. You will not take my stallions, too. No!"

"I did not take your sons, Mendez. I had nothing to do with it."

"Your country."

"Because your country had no jobs for them. Diego, please. Be reasonable. The horse will die here. He will very probably die if I take him. But maybe not. There is a chance. Give it to him."

Diego turned away and stared into the distance.

Paulo held his breath. In his mind a decision was forming. If Danza went to America . . .

Diego turned back. "A loan. I will loan him to you. If he lives he will still belong to me and when I want him back you will send him."

"But you'll let me keep him for at least one breeding season if he should get well enough?"

There was a pause. Paulo held his breath.

Slowly Diego nodded. As the men reached to shake hands Paulo said, "I'm going with him."

# Seven

"No," Diego thundered. "I won't lose you, too."

Paulo stared, surprised by the underlayers of emotion in the old man's voice. "But why would you care if I went? I've never done one single thing right around here. Look what I did to Danza."

Diego turned his stony face away.

Through the kitchen window Paulo heard his mother's voice. "Hello? I need to talk to Ramon Camacho, please. In the maintenance department."

Major Kessler said, "Mr. Mendez, will it be all right if I unload my mares and turn them into your pasture for a few hours? I'll need to go to Maricao for some things. Paulo, Res, want to come along and help?"

The rest of the day was so full of movement that the question of Paulo's leaving was set aside for the time being. The major and the boys unloaded the mares from the truck; then, while Paulo admired the mares' obvious quality, Major Kessler made some phone calls to the Air Transport Office at the San Juan Airport and to the airport in New Orleans.

When he emerged from the house he motioned the boys into the truck.

"Where are we going?" Paulo asked.

"Maricao. We're going to have to rig a portable

sling for Danza. We'll need a welding shop that can do a job in a hurry, and we'll need some strong webbing, something to use for padding—sheepskin or something like that. And we'll have to find somebody with a winch and tackle, maybe a wrecker truck. And Paulo . . ."

"Yes?"

"I'm glad you want to come with Danza. He'll need a round-the-clock nurse, and I won't have time to do it. And you love him. Sometimes that can make the difference between life and death, when it's this close a contest. You've got a job with me for as long as you want it. And of course I'll take care of your travel expenses. I'd already hired a horse transport plane with a twelve-horse capacity, and they allow two passengers to go along with the horses, to take care of them. So your plane fare is no problem. But . . . will your grandfather be a problem?"

Paulo shook his head grimly.

Res said, "It's not fair that you get to go and I don't. I'm the one that's been wanting to, and you never did, Paulo. It doesn't seem right."

Paulo stared wordlessly at the passing scenery. Now that he was committed to leaving, it was more than he could bear to look out at this overwhelmingly familiar countryside rolling away in valley-waves to the distant sea. All of the memories of his fourteen years of life were set in this place.

It was almost supper time when they reached home. Ramon's Buick was parked beside the house. They had dropped Res off in the village, where he had a friend with a brother with a tow truck, and now the tow truck roared into the yard, spewing gravel, just behind the major's rented horse van.

Ramon came down the porch steps as Paulo and Major Kessler alighted. Fidelina and the young children followed.

"Well, Paul. What's this I hear, you want to go to the States with the major?"

"With Danza. I have to. I have to take care of him, Papa. I was the one that made him sick."

Ramon's long, lean face was a study in conflicting emotions. "I know how you feel about the horse, but we have no money for plane tickets. And your grandfather says Danza will likely die anyway. I don't know—"

Major Kessler interrupted. "His plane fare is taken care of, Mr. Camacho, and I'll be taking care of Paulo. He'll be working for me and I'll see that he's all right. He'll be living at my farm, and going to school later on."

Ramon looked from Paulo's face to the major's. "Well, then, it's all right with me, if it's what Paulo wants."

Paulo's feelings were as much in conflict as his father's. Permission was granted. He felt cut adrift from his family. Frightened. Excited. There was an electric trembling in his limbs.

The major moved to his side and dropped a hand on Paulo's shoulders and, steadied by the man's grip, Paulo's trembling diminished and died.

"Come on, Assistant, we have work to do." The major turned Paulo toward the truck.

Everyone helped, Res and his friend and the brother

with the tow truck, Ramon and Manny. Everyone but Diego, who was nowhere in sight. They lowered the ramp on the back of the truck and rolled out the contraption in which Danza would be transported to America.

It was a low platform on dolly wheels. Rising from its corners were stout iron posts well braced and cross-braced. Each post was topped by a heavy iron ring to which were attached webbing straps covered with sheepskin. Pale gold lines of fresh welding caught the light from the setting sun, as the rig was pushed and pulled toward Danza's pen.

The tow truck was backed into position just outside the pen. Res and his friend rigged a pulley, strung with cable, to a beam in the shed roof just above Danza. While they did that, Major Kessler knelt and wrapped the raw stumps of Danza's front feet with dressing and thickly padded bandages bought from the *farmacia* in Maricao.

"All right, now, let's get that bellyband under him if we can." The major's voice rang with authority, and several pairs of hands fell to, shoving and rolling the gaunt blue-gray creature from side to side until the sheepskin-covered band was positioned at Danza's girth.

"Now. Lower that cable. Crank it on down here. Grab the hook, there, Res, get it through the loops on the band. Little more slack. That's it. Okay, now, crank her up, little bit at a time now. Paulo, grab those two loops of webbing for his hind legs. There you go. See if you can slip one around his leg. No, up higher. Clear up."

The cable tautened, and Danza, like a sack of

bones, began to rise from the ground where he had lain for four weeks.

As his body lifted, hand-sized chunks of skin came away from his shoulder and hip and remained stuck to the ground, leaving huge patches of raw meat on the horse's underside.

Paulo's ears began ringing at the sight, and dizziness threatened.

Sharply Major Kessler said, "We'll take care of those in a minute. Hand me that other loop—I've got to get it around this underside hind leg. Keep cranking, fellows, slow but sure, now. Here he comes."

Paulo's dizziness receded in the excitement of seeing Danza suspended in near-standing position. Under the major's directions the iron-rigged platform was rolled under Danza and the webbing harness transferred to the rings atop the platform's corner posts. Danza's hind legs rested lightly on the platform, but most of his weight was suspended in web loops that encircled each hind leg just under his body, so that there was no pressure on his abdomen. His bandaged forefeet, which now resembled giant cotton swabs, were suspended just above the platform.

Danza's head hung low. His eyes drooped. He had no strength to fight this.

The major thanked and paid the tow truck brothers, then turned to Paulo. "You go on in and pack your things, Paulo. I'll take care of Danza's bedsores. Then we'll have to be getting started. The transport plane has to be back tomorrow. Res, if you and your friends would help me get my mares loaded, and Danza up on the truck—"

Paulo turned and ran for the house, suddenly glad that the preparations were moving so swiftly. There'd be no time to say good-bye to Twenty or the stallions. Barely time to say good-bye to his family and to pack a suitcase. No time for thinking, or letting the tears come.

In half an hour the truck was loaded and Paulo was sitting in the front seat. He waved more good-byes and listened to his mother calling one last time, "You write to us every week, you hear? You be good, we love you."

The truck roared to life and began to coast down the road.

Diego did not come to say good-bye. Paulo strained his eyes, and finally caught sight of the old man standing far out in the mare pasture, his back toward the road.

"Bye, Grandfather," Paulo called in a thin voice that was lost in the roar of the truck.

Through the four-hour flight from San Juan to New Orleans Major Kessler slept in the passenger seat just behind the cockpit. Paulo tried to sleep, but there was too much tension in him. He sat on a hay bale that was jammed across the narrow tie stall in which Danza's sling had been rolled, to prevent the contraption from rolling out into the aisle if the flight became rough. Paulo's back was against one of the corner irons of the sling, and Danza's head rested somewhat awkwardly in his lap.

Paulo stroked the hairless skin of Danza's face and wondered if they were killing the horse now, he and the major, by putting him through this traveling.

The sky was streaked with pale dawn-green when they landed at New Orleans. A hired horse van with two drivers was waiting. The two men, and Paulo and the major, walked the nine mares in a grassy area near some old commercial hangars, giving the mares a chance to stretch their legs before they were loaded in the waiting truck.

A veterinarian, an equine specialist from the state university, arrived while the mares were being walked. Major Kessler met the man and shook his hand. "Good morning, sir. I'm Major Kessler, talked to you on the phone. I certainly appreciate your coming out here like this, at such an early hour and all. But the horse is in critical condition. Here he is."

Four airport cargo handlers were lowering Danza in his contraption on a giant forklift.

The veterinarian wasted no time in talking, but began checking Danza's vital signs, temperature, pulse, heartbeat. He opened Danza's mouth and pressed his thumbnail against the horse's gums, then frowned at the length of time the area remained white before the blood returned to the dented area.

"Dehydrated. Starving. Don't know what internal damage might have been done. He must have run a whale of a fever, to have lost his coat and sloughed off his hooves like that."

As he worked he gave Danza glucose and vitamin injections, and antibiotics. Then he whipped out a note pad and wrote on it, and handed the page to the major.

"These ingredients, mixed in these proportions and soaked in hot water; directions are on there. Give it to him every two hours at first. You may only be able to get a cup or so down him at a time, but this is high-concentrate, high-energy food. If he'll eat it at all, and if his digestive system isn't too badly damaged to utilize the nutrients, he should start picking up weight before long.

"Watch those bandages on those front feet. Make sure they're not so tight that they're restricting the blood flow. I'd change them every couple of days if I were you. If he lives, the hooves will start growing back."

"Should we keep him in the sling?" Major Kessler asked.

The man frowned and pinched his bottom lip. "Try it for a while. It might be too much of a strain for him, but on the other hand a horse wasn't designed to eat or drink lying down. He may digest better in an upright position. Oh, and if you've got the time, it would help a lot if you could massage those legs, get the circulation going so those muscles don't atrophy. Massage him all over, neck muscles, hindquarters, everything that's going to have to support him later on. If he lives."

Paulo could keep still no longer. "Do you think he will? Live?"

The man shrugged. "You wouldn't think it to look at him. But I've seen a lot of hopeless-looking animals come back when you'd swear they were gone. It's going to depend an awful lot on this particular horse's guts. His will to live. And that I can't answer for."

On the drive north Paulo's exhaustion overcame his tension and he slept. He and the major rode in the major's car, which he had left at the airport a month before. It was huge and white and glorious, with velvety maroon seats and carpet on the floors.

"You must be rich," Paulo murmured as he sank into the softness of the car's seat. He leaned his head back and closed his eyes.

Major Kessler glanced at the boy with fond amusement and laughed, but Paulo was already asleep.

They drove steadily north, the big white sedan and the bulky horse van, through shimmering green swamplands, past ghost forests of towering cypress killed by encroaching saltwater from the ocean. They slowed for tiny towns of unpainted wooden shacks. They passed endless cotton fields where slat-sided cabins stood above the ground on flimsy pillars.

For lunch they stopped at a highway truck stop and Paulo had his first hamburger. Having slept through the breakfast stop and missing supper last night, he was overwhelmingly hungry and decided the hamburger was the best food he'd ever eaten.

After the lunch stop, the scenery began to change. The land was rising now, and more and more often the car passed through stands of magnificent pines.

"What is your place like?" Paulo asked finally. His mind was full of questions, had been every since yesterday when he knew he was coming here, but he hesitated to speak. Back home the major had seemed to Paulo to be a friendly figure, a lone Americano against the backdrop of Paulo's world—an intelligent, kind man who for some reason seemed to hold Paulo in respect.

But now they were in the major's ball park and Paulo was the foreigner. The lone Puerto Rican boy in a place where he didn't yet belong and maybe never would. In the sudden reversal of positions Paulo felt small beside the major, small and unsure of his worth.

Major Kessler seemed to hear some of Paulo's uncertainty in the boy's voice. He threw Paulo a warm smile and clutched Paulo's knee for an instant, giving it a shake.

"It's a nice place. You'll like it, I think. Couple hundred acres along a little river, mostly pasture and pine forest. I've hired a nice young couple to manage the place for me, and you'll live with them for the time being."

"Where will you be?" Paulo failed to disguise the quaver in his voice.

"I live in Shreveport, Paulo. I'll be out just about every day, though, to see—"

"But I thought you—I thought I'd be living with you—that you retired from the navy to raise horses. I thought that was your big dream."

Even to Paulo his words sounded illogical and overemotional. But to be abandoned like this . . .

"It is my dream, and it will be my main business once it gets going. But my wife is just not a country person. She's spent the last twenty years living wherever the navy sent me, so now it's only fair that she should have a chance to live the way she wants to. All her family and friends are in Shreveport, and that's where she wants to be. It's only a sixty-mile drive. I'll be at the farm most of the time, don't you worry."

Paulo relaxed.

Some time later they turned off the highway onto a

narrow, winding dirt road that seemed to be following the twisting course of an invisible river. They turned again and the car slowed.

This road was no more than a double track of sand tunneling through a dense forest of loblolly pines and water oak. A tangle of vines covered the ground and crept up tree trunks, giving the place an unearthly aura. It was enough like his own forest at home to give Paulo an oddly mixed feeling of loss and of comfort.

He sat up and leaned forward.

Ahead, the tree tunnel opened into brilliant green and gold, a sun-drenched meadow sloping away ahead and to the left. On the right, a house stood just at the edge of the forest. It was a rambling structure of varnished logs, with windows made of glass. A deep porch covered two sides.

As Paulo climbed out of the car a Llewellen setter rose from the porch, stretched, and came to greet him. While the dog was taking inventory of the scents on Paulo's pant legs, a man and woman appeared from the buildings beyond the house.

"You brought horses!" The woman's shout was joyous, and she broke into a run.

"Brought more than that," the major said. "Dennis, Jan, this is Paulo Camacho. He's going to be helping out with the horses, one horse in particular. Paulo, this is Dennis and Janice Crow. Down that way," he said suddenly to the men in the horse van, which had come more slowly than the car over the sandy woods road.

He motioned the truck toward a corral and they all followed.

Paulo looked sideways at these people with whom

he would be living. They seemed young, even from the viewpoint of Paulo's fourteen years. The man had a bush of sandy hair that circled his face in a wreath of a beard and made the rest of him look disproportionately narrow by comparison. His eyes were frank and friendly.

The woman was as tall and as bushy-haired as her husband, and as kind-faced. They both wore jeans and t-shirts, and her hair was tied back from her face by what looked to Paulo like baling twine. Both had sweat-streaked faces and bits of wood chips in their hair.

If they had questions about Paulo's unannounced appearance in their lives, they didn't ask.

"How many were you able to get?" Dennis asked as the van men whanged open the rear door of the truck.

"Nine good mares," Major Kessler said, "and a stallion of sorts. On loan. If he lives."

The two bushy heads turned toward one another, questioning, then toward Paulo. But he didn't notice. He strained to see into the dark van as mare after mare was let out.

*Be still alive,* he prayed silently.

"Oh, look at the pinto," Janice said. "Isn't she pretty? And the black. And the bays. Oh, I love them all. Will it be okay if I ride them, Major Kessler?"

His answer was lost to Paulo as Danza came into view on creaking wheels. Alive! Hang-headed and sagging in his sling, but more alert of eye than he had been for days.

"My God," Dennis said. "What's that!"

"That," Major Kessler said, "is our foundation stallion."

# *Eight*

To Paulo's surprise, the days that followed were to be among the best in his life.

He was given a small bedroom in the log house, the first place he had ever had that was not shared with brothers. It was a good room with bunk beds and a bright rag rug, and a glass window that looked out into the arms of an ancient magnolia tree. But he spent almost no time in his room, nor in the bright gingham kitchen, nor the plank-walled living room with its stone fireplace.

Danza's stall was Paulo's home. He slept there for the first several nights, on Dennis's air mattress and sleeping bag. Beside him, close enough to touch in the night, the gray form of Danza hung in its sling.

The stable, which was made of pine logs like the house, was so newly built that the carpenters were still at work building and hanging the stall doors that moved on silent rollers and fascinated Paulo. During the daytime the workmen were company for Paulo, their voices and their radio, and their curious kind interest in Danza's progress.

And progress it was, from the first day, from the first

feeding of the warm mash the New Orleans veterinarian had prescribed. A Shreveport veterinarian came out with Major Kessler the day after Danza's arrival, but he only seconded the original plan of treatment and shook his head sadly at the pitiful sight of Danza.

Every two hours Paulo mixed the grains to make the mash, poured hot water over it from the little stove in the stable's raw new office, covered it to steam, then offered it to Danza, first in his hand and later, as the horse's appetite gathered strength, in the bucket.

Between feedings Paulo massaged the stringy muscles in Danza's legs as the Shreveport veterinarian had showed him, and moved the dangling front legs back and forth, back and forth in a simulated walking motion. He tended the bandaged feet and the open bedsores along Danza's side, and he rubbed baby oil into the blue-gray skin that covered Danza's skeleton.

Sometimes he napped between feedings. Sometimes he wandered up to the house to get something to eat or drink, or to use the beautiful inside bathroom.

For the first time in his life Paulo knew the heady feeling of being in charge of himself. Danza's needs were all he had to answer to. About mid-morning each day Major Kessler arrived and came directly to Danza's stall. His appearance was the day's high point for Paulo.

"I believe he's holding his head up higher, Paulo," the major would say, or, "He's filling out. See that little pad of flesh he's getting between his spine and the curve of his ribs? You're doing a fine job, Paulo."

The words, the smile in the man's eyes, were a balm

to Paulo. So long he had waited for his father to notice him. So long he had hoped for words of praise from his grandfather, had built daydreams around it even. Now the major's approval came down on him like winter sunshine, and he unfolded and grew in it.

During those first two weeks when Paulo was seldom out of sight of the horse, the closeness that had always existed between them took on a new depth. Sometimes it seemed to Paulo that their very breathing was in unison. Paulo found that he was able to sleep deeply only at times when Danza slept and Danza's waking, silent though it was, woke Paulo in the same instant.

One night Paulo dreamed that his fingernails had grown long and were maddeningly itchy in the tender flesh just beneath them. The next day when he cut away Danza's foot bandages he saw a ridge of new hoof appearing at the coronet band.

When he showed it to Janice and Major Kessler a little later, the major said, "That calls for a celebration. Paulo, you've been cooped up in here long enough without a break. Let's go for a ride. Janice, you come, too, and let's take sandwiches. How long till Danza's next feeding, Paulo?"

"Four hours. He's up to four-hour feedings now, and I just did him. Two o'clock will be the next. Can we really?"

"You bet your shinbone. Let's get a move on."

They chose three of the mares that Janice had discovered to be broken to ride—the pinto who was already Janice's favorite, a bay for Paulo, and a large liver chestnut mare for the major. Dennis, who was more farmer than horseman, waved them away cheerfully and went back to his fence building.

It was a perfect September day, just past the worst of the summer's heat. A pine-scented breeze billowed Paulo's shirt and lifted his mare's mane. They set out at a brisk corto across the meadow, the mares all full of dance. The breeze rippled the deergrass and showed flashes of color where asters and ground orchids bloomed.

Janice turned to Paulo, her face glowing with pleasure. "Boy, this sure beats trotting. I just love these Paso Finos."

Paulo grinned. "I never rode a horse that trotted. What's it like?"

"Bumpy. If you ride English you have to post to it, to keep from getting jounced to death. That means kind of standing up in the stirrups every other beat and it gets pretty tiring after while. Or if you ride western you just have to sit the trot and try not to bounce around too much."

Paulo pondered the strangeness of this big rich country where people who could obviously afford anything they wanted contented themselves with horses that trotted.

The major, who had been riding behind the other two in order to enjoy the sight of his mares, caught up and said, "Paulo, you'll have to help me think of names for these mares, since you're bilingual. Most of them just had numbers, and we want to get them registered in the American registry, so . . ."

"Since I'm what?"

"Bilingual. You speak two languages equally well. Spanish and English."

"Oh. Sure. Lots of people do, at home. You're going to name the mares, huh?" He grinned.

Janice looked at him quizzically. "Why wouldn't he?"

"Oh," Paulo shrugged, "down there we don't usually. And we don't ride them. At least, men don't." He shot a sidelong glance at the major, who rode with a calm half-smile on his face, unperturbed at the implied threat to his manhood.

Janice snorted. "Well, that's dumb. You're wasting half of your horses that way. And besides, if you didn't have mares you couldn't have future generations. We prize a good mare here, don't we, major?"

"Yes, indeed. And a good gelding. But I will have to agree with Paulo's viewpoint to a certain extent. A fine stallion is still the epitome of equine magnificence."

Paulo was embarrassed that he didn't understand all those words, but the embarrassment melted away in the glow of the major's aligning himself with Paulo.

At the far edge of the meadow they found a timber road that led through a forest of pines so tall and straight and dense that their upper branches blocked out all sunlight. The trunks rose cleanly for thirty feet before the branches began, and the forest floor was bare of underbrush. Foot-thick blankets of pine needles covered the ground and drifted across the road so that the horses' feet made swishing sounds as they ambled along.

They came to a small river, and stopped there to eat their sandwiches and to rest the horses. The water was so clear that the sandy bottom seemed illuminated and magnified. Silver fish darted through the shadows near the banks.

The talk was easy and pleasant. Paulo rested his head against the tree trunk behind him and thought that this day, the perfection of it, would stay in his memory even when he was an old man.

It was just a few days later that Paulo felt stubble beneath his palm when he began Danza's morning massage. When the sun rose above the pines and slanted in through the window in Danza's stall it illuminated a faint cast of red over the horse's body. Seen head-on, the new hairs were almost invisible, but at an angle they showed up, so the ridges and contours of Danza's body seemed shaded red as though he had been outlined by a child's crayon. A line of black traced the ridge of Danza's neck.

The animal's ravaged system was finally sufficiently healed and nourished that it could divert energy from survival and use it to produce hair.

"He's got hair!" Paulo ran out of the stable, shouting.

Once they'd begun, Danza's hooves and coat grew back with exciting speed. Every morning Paulo ran from the house, where he slept now that the crisis was past, to Danza's stall in the fragrant new stable. Each day the red sheen of Danza's coat was more and more apparent, and eventually the blue-gray skin was covered. Coltish tufts of mane crested Danza's neck, and his tailbone was at last decently, if briefly, covered with a brush of tail hair.

His hooves, within their bandages, grew at a rate much faster than normal hooves would have grown, as was typical with founder hooves. Gradually, as week followed week through October and November, the hooves approached ground level, encasing the gristly inner tissue of Danza's feet.

Paulo's schedule shifted with the lessening of Danza's dependence on him. He was out of his bunk bed and out of the house even earlier than Dennis and Janice, so that he could give Danza a good hour of attention before the morning chores began. He fed his horse, normal rations of hay and grain by now, cleaned his stall, massaged his muscles, and rubbed him all over with a terrycloth towel, gentler than a brush on the thin new coat and yet invigorating to the circulation of Danza's blood. He checked often for sores under the webbing of the sling.

Then Paulo and Janice gave each of the nine mares a light grooming and a thorough stall cleaning while Dennis carted in bales of hay and bedding, and buckets of grain. Then breakfast and a hike out to the main road in time to meet the school bus. Back home by four for the best part of the day, riding two or three of the mares for as long as time permitted, in the oval training ring that was being completed beyond the stable. Evening chores and more massaging for Danza's legs, then a late supper, a sleepy hour or two of homework, and deep exhausted sleep.

At first the school had terrified Paulo. He was a month late in starting because of Danza's need for frequent feeding. It was a strange school full of Americano children, and the subjects they studied were in some cases new to Paulo. But the major looked down at him with calm eyes and expected him to make this leap into the new school, so Paulo did it. And by Christmastime he realized that he had been absorbed into the class. He caught up, or was catching up in most subjects and was well ahead of most of the boys in his ability to handle a baseball. He was finally able to relax and to cease dreading each new school day.

The homesickness that came and went in Paulo through the autumn months intensified during the Christmas holidays. It seemed wrong to him to be exchanging gifts on December 25 instead of Three Kings' Day, January 6. But his gift from Janice and Dennis was a phone call home, and that helped.

Odd though, he thought as he hung up the phone, how far away they all seemed down there in Puerto Rico; how much more real his life in this Louisiana pine forest had become to him. It was fun describing Danza's progress and his own increased activities at school, but Paulo was somewhat surprised at his own lack of interest in the family's news.

By mid-January Danza was free of his sling. He stood on new-grown hooves that were adequate to support his weight on soft surfaces, on legs pitifully thin in comparison to his body, which had the look, now, of a normal but thin horse. In spite of Paulo's relentless massaging, six months of disuse had shrunk Danza's leg muscles nearly to nonexistence.

"But he'll be able to breed," the major said with a ringing satisfaction as he stood with Paulo looking over Danza's stall door. "The mares will start cycling around March, but we'll give him till, say, April, to build up his strength. What we need to do now, Paulo, is to get him out of this stall; give him as much exercise as you can. Keep him on soft surfaces, of course, but walk him. In the training ring, on grass, maybe in the woods on those nice soft pine needles when he gets strong enough to go that far. Okay?"

"You bet."

And what's going to happen, then? Paulo wondered after the major wandered away down the stable aisle. What happens after you've got your season's breeding that Grandfather promised you, and your mares are all carrying Danza's foals. Does he go back to Puerto Rico?

Do I?

He wasn't sure whether he wanted to go home or not. Dennis and Janice treated him fondly and comfortably, as though he were a younger brother. The major's visits were something to look forward to, and of course Danza was the center of Paulo's existence.

It wasn't home, but it was nice here.

The spring air was thick with fragrances—the magnolia and dogwood trees around the house, jasmine and wild azalea and silverbells in the meadow. Even the grass had a lush green scent under their feet as Paulo and Danza strolled up the sloping meadow toward the training ring. Paulo's hands were in his pockets, the lead rope draped casually through his arm.

Danza looked a bit like a small Quarter horse; a six-inch mane lay on his neck. His tail reached his hocks. His ribs had disappeared and there was a gloss on his gold-red coat. Only the thinness of his legs and neck and the fact that he was walking instead of traveling in his usual fino-prance gave away the fact of his convalescence.

They paused beside the training ring fence to watch Janice and Miel, a sturdy little palomino mare whom Paulo had named for the honey color of her coat and the sweetness of her nature. Miel was the only one of the nine mares who showed a talent for the fino form of the gait, and since the major had begun talking about the horse shows that were now being held by the newly formed breed organization, Janice had been working every spare minute on Miel.

Paulo rested his chin on his arm and squinted at the pair who were circling the ring. He shook his head slightly and said to Danza, "She just doesn't quite have it. She doesn't know how to ride a fino horse. That little mare's just dogging along."

Danza arched his neck over the fence and watched the mare, his ears stiff with interest.

"Touch up her head," Paulo called. "She's getting too strung out."

"What do you mean, 'Touch up her head'?" Janice called. She was sweating with effort, and the band that held back her hair threatened to slip down over her eyes.

"I can't explain it. Just, well, gather her up."

Janice tightened the reins and Miel halted. She moved foward again when Janice pressed with her legs, but she moved nervously, unsure of what was wanted of her.

Paulo's hands moved forward into rein-holding position. His wrists ached for the play of the horse's mouth through those delicate leather telegraph lines.

Janice and Miel halted in front of Paulo. "I don't know, Paulie. I don't seem to have much of a knack for fino-ing. Maybe I'd be better off sticking with the corto-largo horses. I'm afraid of messing her up. Here, let me watch you do it again."

She slipped off and exchanged her reins for Danza's lead rope. Grinning, Paulo settled himself in the saddle and collected the reins.

Miel flicked her ears. The touch on her mouth was light but steady. Reassuring. She felt herself pushed forward by her rider's legs and seat bones. Smoothly she shifted her weight forward and arched her neck so that the gentle pressure of bit against her bars became something dependable against which she could balance and steady herself. She moved around the ring in a tidy fino, not too fast and with good brio-snap at the pasterns.

As he came back toward Janice Paulo looked toward her, then looked again and brought Miel to a halt.

Danza was glaring at Paulo, his ears flattened, his tail lashing angrily. Although he was standing in place, his feet were lifting in a perfect fino rhythm.

Janice looked, too, and laughed. "Would you look at him? He's jealous. He doesn't like you riding another horse, I bet."

Still staring at Danza, Paulo dropped to the ground and handed Miel back to Janice. His fingers closed around Danza's lead rope but he felt nothing. Danza's eye, so close to the boy's face, seemed to beam a challenge that seared through Paulo's caution.

I'm ready, Danza told him with the movement of his hooves and the arch of his neck, with the flicking of his black-rimmed ears and all the intensity of facial expression an intelligent horse can produce.

111

It was time. Paulo knew it more certainly than if the veterinarian had pronounced the words.

He led Danza into the ring, flung the lead rope over the horse's neck, and jumped. As he settled onto Danza's back a wash of fear went through him. The legs, were they really ready? Was he hurting Danza?

But the horse began to move, and Paulo knew it was right. He relaxed as the glory of the moment stung his eyes to dampness.

Eight months, first of living in fear that Danza would die, then in fear that he would never walk again nor carry Paulo, the grueling, grinding weariness of caring for the wrecked creature hanging in his sling— it all faded like smoke in the air as Danza began to fino.

The beat was muffled to a soft patter, but Paulo felt, in the marrow of his bones, the rhythm of Danza's steps. He felt, too, the tremor in the weakened legs.

As they circled the ring Miel and Janice fell into step beside them. The red-gold stallion and the cream-and-honey mare flowed around the dusty oval in a dance that was centuries old.

# Nine

On a Friday afternoon two weeks later a dark green truck and trailer descended the arc of a three-mile-long Mississippi River bridge and leveled itself for the pull to Jackson. The truck was a pickup, but of mammoth proportions and with a back seat. The trailer was a four-horse gooseneck with sleeping facilities, tack, feed, and dressing rooms.

The signs on the truck doors said, *Paso Pines, A. J. Kessler.* The freshly done lettering on the flanks of the trailer said, *Paso Fino Horses, The Horse With The Cadillac Ride.*

Major Kessler smiled as he drove. Paulo sat beside him, taking an occasional drink from a Coke can, and Janice lay on the back seat trying to nap but being continually drawn into the conversation.

"I can't figure you out," Paulo said. "You own these horses. They're yours. How come you don't ride them yourself? How come you got me and Jan to do your riding for you?"

The major's grin widened. "You do it better than I do."

"Hah," Janice said from the back.

"Well, Paulo does it better than I could anyway, and you do at least as well as I could with the pinto mare, Jan. And it's obvious by now that neither one of us can get the showing out of Miel that Paulo can."

Paulo said, with somewhat forced modesty, "It takes years of practice to be a good fino rider. And it helps if you're born Latin."

Janice chuckled and the major said, "So all right. I'd be hampering my horses' chances of winning if I insisted on doing the riding just because I owned them."

Paulo just shook his head. An incredibly strange country. People owning horses that other people can ride better than they can themselves. And driving so far to go to a horse show that you have to stay overnight when you get there, and all that for a show in which only six classes are for Paso Finos and all the other classes are for other kinds of horses. And showing mares. And spending more on a truck and trailer than on any of the horses.

"I don't think I'll ever get the hang of this place," he muttered. "Nobody goes this far for a horse show in Puerto Rico."

Janice raised one foot and tipped Paulo's hat forward over his face. "If you drove this far in Puerto Rico you'd fall into the ocean."

They laughed and the talk drifted on, but Paulo's thoughts were snagged on Puerto Rico. Three of the major's nine mares were now bred to Danza, and the others would be within the next month or so. Major Kessler had said nothing yet about when he would be returning Danza, and Paulo, to Diego. If there had been correspondence between the two men on the matter, Paulo knew nothing about it. He found himself curiously neutral. To go home with Danza, to resume his life with Diego's horses, or to stay here with Danza and continue with the major's horses—it hardly seemed to matter, so long as Danza was in the center of his life.

They arrived at the show grounds in the late afternoon. Paulo was stunned at the size of the place and at the number of rigs as big as the major's and bigger. And fancier. There were rows of huge white barns and four show rings bigger than any he had ever imagined. Two of them were crisscrossed with fake fences, bridges, hedges.

"Those are for the jumping classes," Janice explained as their truck rolled slowly past the rings.

They got their barn assignments and unloaded Miel and Bobo, the pinto mare. The stalls were big and luxuriously bedded. While Paulo and Janice saw to the horses' needs, the major strolled through the section assigned to Paso Finos, introducing himself to other exhibitors, shaking hands, admiring their horses. Within minutes he was involved in an impromptu party in one of the exhibitors' tack stalls where a portable bar was set up.

Paulo watched from a little distance, and tried not to feel like a hired stable hand. He wanted to join the group. He wanted the major to remember him and *invite* him to join the group.

Jan came up behind him and dropped her arm good-naturedly across his shoulders. "Come on, you little hot-shot Latin fino-rider, let's walk around and see the sights."

"You bet."

From barn to barn they went, wandering up one aisle and down the next, peering into stalls and circling around horses cross-tied in their paths. Paulo's eyes opened wide at the size and elegance of the Saddlebreds, and no less so at the fancy blue or purple draperies, white-edged and white-lettered, that curtained off stalls, or rows of stalls, and proclaimed that territory *Townsend Stables*, or *Rolling Hills American Saddlebreds*.

In the next barn Paulo stopped so suddenly Janice ran into him. "What's the matter with that horse's feet?" he whispered, and tried not to stare.

A dark chestnut horse as big and elegant as the Saddlebreds was standing in the aisle having his mane braided. At first glance he seemed to be standing on blocks, but when Paulo looked more closely he could see that the animal's front hooves were simply incredibly long, and ended in what appeared to be rubber shoes two inches thick. In addition, he wore braceletlike chains around his pasterns.

"That's a Tennessee Walking Horse," Jan murmured. "That's the way they show them."

"Why?!"

"All that weight on their front feet makes them pick their feet up high. Makes them look showy."

Paulo just shook his head.

"Boy, you Americans are a crazy bunch."

"Well, not all of us," she said defensively.

In the next barn were Morgans and Arabians. Paulo's eyes lit up with pleasure at the beauty of the

116

horses. "Some of them are almost as good-looking as Danza," he said as they left to start back toward their own barn.

Janice laughed and said, "You know, don't you, that every single horse owner here is just as sold on his own breed as we are on Pasos. And all of these breeds are the best at something or other."

"How come you know so much? You been to lots of these horse shows?"

"Every chance I've had, since I was a little kid. But I could never have a horse of my own. Could never afford it. So this will be my first time to ride in a show."

"Big deal, huh?"

"Yeah."

They grinned at each other.

"There you are," Major Kessler called from the door of their barn. "I've been looking for you two. Come on, we're all going out for dinner. Here, come here a minute. My chief assistant Paulo Camacho, my other chief assistant Janice Crow, these are the Feldens here, and the Moores, and I've forgotten some of the other names already, but we're all going out for shrimp and lobster."

Paulo glowed.


The sixth class on Saturday morning was Miel's. Classic Fino Open. While Jan did the final grooming and saddling, Paulo fought the cramped dressing space in the trailer and got into his new clothes. Different from his show clothes at home, he kept thinking as he pulled on the slim black pants with their flared legs and

117

silver piping down the sides. The shirt was white and ruffled, and covered at the waist by a black satin cummerbund. The jacket came just to his waist and matched the pants, and he was topped by a flat-brimmed black hat, Spanish-style. The new boots came only to his ankles, but they were surprisingly comfortable.

Miel danced toward the ring on polished hooves. Her mane and tail were spun silver and her coat fairly glared in the sun. She was a small mare, barely 13.2 hands, but Paulo's own small stature set her off well, and Paulo knew they looked good.

He tried to concentrate on Miel, but other thoughts slipped in: So different. Such a big ring and only that little bit of audience. This is a big city. Where are all the people? Don't they know there's a horse show going on? Don't they come out to cheer for their local horses, like at home? Boy, this is a funny country.

Miel placed fourth in the class of nine, and those who placed above her were all stallions, bigger and more impressive than little Miel. Paulo was pleased with the fourth-place ribbon, but as he left the ring and handed it to Major Kessler, the man's face was impassive.

"Pretty good, for a mare against stallions," Paulo ventured as he dismounted and handed Miel to Janice.

"Yes. Nice job." The words were perfunctory.

After lunch Janice got into her show suit, identical to Paulo's, and rode Bobo in the Performance and Pleasure classes. Paulo and the major watched from the bleachers. The Performance class was huge. Twenty horses, and all of them classier than Bobo,

Paulo thought as he watched. They performed the corto, the largo, a flat walk, then reversed direction and repeated the gaits. The horses moved with precision, style, and elegance that surprised Paulo. For such importance to be placed on corto-largo horses seemed strange to him. At shows at home, the corto-largo classes were considered unimportant. Only the Bella Forma classes on long lines, and the fino classes for the pure beauty of the parade gait, would have drawn entries this big, and horses of this quality.

He was not surprised that Jan and Bobo were among the first group of horses to be excused from the ring so that the horses who were serious contenders would have more room to perform.

A man sitting on the other side of Major Kessler, and to whom the major had been talking, said, "What you need is a professional trainer, major. That's a nice enough little mare, but your rider just isn't getting a performance out of her. Same with your palomino in the Classic Fino class this morning."

Paulo bristled.

"You think so?" the major said.

"Um. If you want to be on top in this business. I've been in Pasos five years now, about as long as anybody in this country, and I know what I'm talking about. They're a coming breed. When the American public finds out about them they're going to be the hottest thing in pleasure horses this country has ever seen. And the show ring competition is going to get just as tough as it is in Saddlebreds and Walking Horses, and the western breeds in other parts of the country. Even at this little show, you watch. It's the professionals that'll

119

be copping top honors in the important classes, like Performance and Fino and Bella Forma."

Paulo sizzled at the implication that any rider here was more professional a rider than he was on a Paso Fino.

Major Kessler pinched his lip. "It bears considering. We just brought these two mares for fun, for a little ring experience. But I've got a stallion at home, he's been sick and he's not in show condition quite yet, but another month or so and he should make a top contender in Fino. I'd like him to have every advantage . . ."

Paulo stared, gape-mouthed. Danza? The major would show Danza, and put some other rider on him? But Danza's feet, his legs—could they take the strain? And how could the major even consider letting anyone else ride Danza? Paulo steamed.

The Paso Pleasure class came into the ring, Bobo and Janice among them. Although many of the horses were the same as in the Performance class, they were ridden in a more relaxed way now. There was less collection to their carriage, and their strides were long, smoother, in response to their riders' attitudes. In selecting for qualities that made for a safe and pleasant ride rather than for spirit and flash, the judge looked more kindly toward Bobo, and placed her sixth.

Janice radiated delight as she came out of the ring, but Paulo hardly saw her.

On the drive home, the major's subdued mood spread to Paulo and Janice. Major Kessler was disappointed in the showing his horses had made and they both knew it. Glancing sideways Paulo could see ridges of tensed muscle in the major's jaw.

A few days later Major Kessler appeared at Danza's stall door. Paulo was hunched over Danza's near front hoof, scraping gently across the sole with a hoof pick.

"How's it look?" the major asked.

Paulo turned. "Hi. Looks healthy enough, on the sole anyway." He ran his thumb over the unnaturally rough surface of the hoof wall. "But he gets pretty tenderfooted if I have to even cross a gravel road with him. And his leg muscles are still a long way from what they should be."

The major pinched his lip and frowned. "Two months from now, what do you reckon?"

"What do you mean?"

"Could he be shown, do you think? One or two classes?"

Paulo dropped the hoof and straightened up. "Who'd be riding him?"

"Probably you. Why, would that make a difference?"

For the first time Paulo felt anger toward the major. "Make a difference? Naturally. In the first place, no professional trainer in this country can get the performance I could out of Danza. He'd never give as much for a stranger. And furthermore than that, I can feel the exact minute his feet start hurting him. If he's in pain I can feel his pain. No stranger is going to be able to tell that first little second when it starts hurting him."

"Yes, well, that makes sense, Paulo. Tell you what, you keep working on him, do whatever you can to get him in condition between now and June, and you can ride him at Baton Rouge. If he does well there, we'll keep showing him, try to get him qualified for the National Championship show in September. I'd like awfully well to win a National Championship in Classic Fino with him. Nothing wrong with aiming for the top, is there?'' The major and Paulo grinned at each other. "That'd get us some respect among the other Paso breeders in the country. And some hefty stud fees.''

When the major left and Paulo was riding Danza in the training ring, Paulo thought, *I guess that means we're going to stay a while, old horse. I wonder about those hefty stud fees. Are they supposed to go to him or to Grandfather?*

He shook his head. The major had become so many important things to Paulo—a father, a friend, a man to admire and pattern himself after. He didn't dare allow himself to think that he might have chosen an unworthy compadre, that the major might be taking advantage of the situation, to make money he might not be entitled to.

April became May, and Danza's workouts gradually lengthened to twenty minutes twice a day in the ring, and hour-long gentle rides in the middle of the day. On these rides Danza went bareback and with just a rope hackamore on his head, and Paulo wore raveling old denim shorts and a shirt so seam-ripped that its only function was to keep the mosquitoes off.

They went across the meadow, which was now fenced for a brood mare pasture, then along the sandy track through the pines to the river. Here, with shared enjoyment, horse and boy sailed into the water, splashing mightily. Only in the center of the channel was it deep enough to support a swimming horse, so Paulo swam Danza up and down that narrow center channel until even that buoyant exercise began to tire the horse.

One afternoon when Paulo and Danza were loafing in the river, idly watching the fish swim by, Danza heard a sudden snapping of twigs from the woods. He threw his head up and shied and Paulo, who had been lying half-asleep on the horse's back, rolled off into the water.

He came up sputtering, and heard a child's laugh. A girl of perhaps twelve sat watching him from the back of a small dappled gray mare.

"You fall off a horse good," she said. "Remember me? I met you at the Jackson show. Marilyn Felden, remember?"

Paulo thrashed his way back up onto Danza so he could talk to her as an equal. With the water out of his eyes he could see the girl more clearly, and she did look familiar.

"Oh, yeah," he said. "What are you doing here?"

"We came up to look at your stallion, and we brought Nibs along in case my dad decided to breed her to him." She pointed down at her mare. "Her name is Bella Niebla. That means Beautiful Mist, in Spanish."

"Look, kid," Paulo flared, "you don't need to tell me Spanish. I'm bilingual. That means I speak two languages equally well."

She accepted that. She had a round face of the kind that smiles easily, straight pale hair, and owlishly large round glasses.

She nodded at Danza. "Is that him?"

"What do you think?"

"Must be him." She shrugged. "The lady at the house told me that you were down here riding him in the river, and I was supposed to come get you. So that must be him."

Paulo waited for her to admire him. She said nothing.

"Well?" he finally snapped.

"Can't see much of him, underwater. Why don't you bring him out? We're supposed to be getting back, anyway."

Paulo drove Danza up over the bank, deliberately close to the girl and her mare, and Danza, as Paulo expected, paused to shake the water off of himself. It arced in a rainbow of drops over the girl and mare, but Marilyn just laughed and said, "Hey, that felt good."

They rode side by side along the sandy track. Paulo gathered Danza's forward thrust against the hackamore and with his legs he squeezed Danza up into a quick-step sideways prance. Danza's neck was tightly arched, his ears snapping forward and back with excitement.

Finally Marilyn said, "He's really pretty."

Paulo relaxed and allowed Danza to relax, too. He said, "You think your dad will like him?"

Marilyn nodded and grinned. "He's been looking all over for a stallion to breed her to. He didn't want one too big, because we like the smaller size Pasos, and he likes bays, and he wanted a fino stallion because somebody told him that a fino stallion will do a better job of purifying the gait than a corto-largo stallion would, if

124

your mare isn't too good in her gaits. And Nibs gets kind of trotty sometimes."

Paulo nodded wisely. "That's right. You couldn't do better than Danza. His sire was Bonanza—you ever heard of him?"

She shook her head, and Paulo sighed at her ignorance.

"He was Puerto Rican Island Champion two years in a row. Danza's dam was the best mare we had. I learned to ride on her. She could fino with the best, and corto and largo, too. She could largo faster than my grandfather's truck could run, just about."

Marilyn absorbed this with polite skepticism and said, "Did Danza ever get to be Island Champion himself?"

"He hasn't had a chance yet," Paulo said hotly. "He got foundered when he was three, and he's been here ever since, getting over it. But I'm going to start showing him next month at Baton Rouge, and you just watch. He'll be Island Champion by the end of the year."

"You mean National Champion?"

"Yeah. That's what I meant."

"Well, good. He better be, for the stud fee Major Kessler is charging."

Paulo said slowly, "Why? How much is he charging?"

"Eight hundred dollars."

"He's worth it," Paulo said, but there was a faintness to his voice. Eight hundred dollars. Ten times what Danza's stud fee would be back home.

Eight hundred dollars going into the major's pocket. The fact was a wound to Paulo.

# *Ten*

The Baton Rouge show was held in an indoor arena, a tanbark oval brightened by overhead lights that threw the stands and the high arched roof into shadows. An unseen organist played "The Tennessee Waltz" in rhythm with the strides of the horses in the ring. It was the Walking Horse Amateur Owner class.

The next class, the last one on the evening's program, was Paso Finos, Open Classic Fino.

Paulo sat on Danza in the waiting area just outside the ring entrance. His continual stroking of the horse's neck was an unconscious attempt to control his own nerves.

So much depended on their doing well tonight. The major had all but spelled it out and Paulo was quick to understand. Danza was to be shown; Danza was to win. If Paulo was capable of getting a winning performance out of him, fine. Otherwise Danza would be put into the hands of a professional trainer.

So much depended on tonight, and so much was wrong. Danza was nervous in this building, with its racketing acoustics and glare of artificial lights. The organ music came too loudly through loudspeakers placed just above the horses' heads as they circled the cramped ring. Paulo himself was jumpy. And, most serious of all, Danza's legs weren't ready.

The weeks of ring workouts, roadwork, and river swimming had filled out the contours of Danza's legs with muscles that appeared normal in size. His hooves appeared as normal as possible, given their rough surface and the abnormally fast growth of founder hooves. They had been carefully trimmed back once a week and watched for impending cracks or chipping away. But Paulo knew there was weakness still in those legs, and tenderness in the hooves.

And he knew, better than Major Kessler or Jan, or the vet or the farrier, the demands that would be made tonight on Danza's legs. He knew that the extreme collection of the fino gait created tension throughout a horse's body, from the tightly arched neck to the undertucked hindquarters, and sustained tension was exhausting. He knew that the quick-snap brio motion in a fino horse's pasterns and fetlock joints, though beautiful to watch and magic to ride, were difficult for the most hardened horse to maintain over a period of time, much less a horse who had so recently spent six months suspended in a sling. He had tried to argue the point with the major, but to no avail.

The Walking Horse class was over. Danza moved aside nervously as the tall nodding horses came out of the gate. The organ music changed to "Spanish Eyes."

Paulo held back until the other five stallions had entered the ring. As they passed him he became aware of another of Danza's disadvantages. His mane and tail. Normal length now for a horse of another breed, but dismayingly skimpy next to the flowing magnificence of the others in the ring.

As the last horse passed him, Paulo lifted his reins and, with his legs, pressed Danza up into his gait and into the ring. For an instant Paulo forgot the shadowy sea of audience faces, the glaring lights, and blaring music. He felt the rhythm of Danza's steps, and it felt right.

He relaxed a fraction, and a smile of pure enjoyment lit his face. This was the center kernal of life, this moment with five thousand Americanos watching him, watching Danza in perfect fino.

Around the ring the six stallions danced; black, bay, chestnut, golden chestnut, mahogany bay, and Danza, bright blood bay. The rustling of the audience grew quiet.

"Reverse please," the announcer called, and six horses circled inward, then continued in the opposite direction without breaking the perfect four-beat cadence of their gait.

After a few more laps of the ring the announcer called for the horses to line up at the far end of the ring. Paulo felt prickles of relief run down his arms. The judge wasn't going to make an endurance trial out of it. Danza would be able to stop now and rest, at least for a little while, and as yet Paulo could feel no tremor of weakening muscles beneath him.

One by one the judge motioned each horse to the center of the ring for a figure eight. He squinted at the flashing legs, watching for a break in the gait as the horses maneuvered the tight turns. Two of the horses did break cadence. Another slowed noticeably as he bent around the corners, and another circled much wider than he should have.

*Good,* Paulo thought.

Danza performed his figure eight perfectly.

Paulo threw a quick grin toward the major, who was watching, tense-faced, near the ring entrance.

The judge marked his sheet and handed it to the ring steward, who bore it across the tanbark to the announcer.

"We have the judge's decision," the announcer trumpeted.

Paulo lifted his hands. Danza collected himself and sidestepped forward.

"First place goes to Selecto, owned by Lookout Mountain Stables, shown by Fred Coulter."

Paulo sagged, then sat up in rising anger. How could any of these horses—oh, well, second then. The major would be satisfied with that.

"Second, number thirty-one, Bolivar, owned and ridden by T.J. Thompson.

"Third, number one-eleven, Danza, owned by Diego Mendez, ridden by Paul Camacho."

Paulo rode forward to collect his rosette. Third. Why? And was that going to be good enough? Would the major . . .

He was out of the ring, out of the building, and into the illuminated night. The road from the stables to the arena was full of horse and foot traffic. The major appeared beside Paulo's stirrup, but there was no time or privacy for words to be exchanged.

In Danza's stall as he unsaddled, Paulo glanced side-long at the major. The man had hung the yellow rosette on Danza's stall door with what appeared to be a proper amount of pride, and he answered the congratulations of the other exhibitors lounging in the aisle with smiles. But Paulo was attuned to this man. He heard the flat tone beneath the repartee.

To Paulo the major said nothing. He rubbed Danza's face with the flat of his palm, but said nothing.

Finally Paulo broke the silence. "We should have won it."

"Do you know why we didn't, Paulo?"

"No. Why?"

"I don't know. I'm asking you. I thought maybe Danza broke gait at some crucial point and I didn't catch it, or something like that. I saw other horses making mistakes, including the two that placed over us."

Paulo shook his head and began sponging off the damp saddle mark on Danza's back. "Beats me. Unless your Americano judges go by the length of a horse's mane."

"Now, don't start getting national about it. I guess it was just one of those decisions that you get sometimes in showing horses. We'll see what happens at Lake Charles week after next."

"Same thing that just happened." It was a new voice. Paulo turned quickly. Marilyn Felden's father stood in the stall door. He was a pleasant-looking man with the round, open face of a farmer, although he was actually a New Orleans importer of gifts and inexpensive art objects.

"Hello, Felden." The major shook hands. "Nice to see you again."

130

Paulo asked, "What did you mean, what you said?"

Mr. Felden pulled in a long breath and stepped into the stall. He reached to stroke Danza's neck. "I meant that you're up against the pros in that class, Paulo. The professional trainers. In Fino competition, especially, you're going to be up against them everywhere you go, and nine times out of ten they're going to have the advantage over you."

Paulo's anger flamed in his face.

"It has nothing to do with your ability," Mr. Felden went on. "Personally, I think you did a fine job tonight, Paulo, as good as any professional could have done with Danza. And I feel sure he was the equal of any horse in that ring. And for my money, if I were judging, I'd give preference to a stallion so well-mannered that a young boy can handle him. But—"

Paulo and the major listened intently.

"What are you, Paulo, eleven? Twelve?"

"Fifteen," Paulo snapped.

"Really?" Mr. Felden looked surprised. "Well, the point is you look like twelve, and when the judges have a ring full of well-known professional trainers, with big reputations in the breed, people the judges know personally, well, they're just not going to take you too seriously. It's not fair, but it's a fact of life."

Beneath his seething anger Paulo felt a cold shaft of realism. After the major left to go out for drinks with the Feldens and some other Paso exhibitors, Paulo stretched out on his bed in the trailer to think about it.

He remembered driving home from a show in Lares.

Bonanza had won a large, quality-packed Fino class, but Diego had driven silently, as though his mind were on something else.

Finally Paulo had ventured, "That was a great win, wasn't it, Grandfather?"

"No. No, it was a win, but not one to be happy about."

"But why not? Thirty-two in the class, and—"

"There was a better horse than Bonanza," Diego said harshly. "The blue roan. He was better."

"But the judge didn't think so, and that's what counts."

Diego turned savagely toward Paulo. "You are a stupid child. It is the horses that matter. Jesus Ramirez gave that win to Bonanza because he's just bred two of his mares to Bonanza and he wants to help make him Island Champion this year to make his own colts more valuable. That's human nature. We're not as honest as the animals we use to make ourselves bigger men."

Paulo was silent for several minutes, then asked in a small voice, "Does it happen a lot? That you get wins when you don't think you should have?"

"Sometimes. Just as often it goes the other way, and the system works against us. We're beaten by someone with better connections, or someone who sores his horses."

"Sores?"

"Hurts their feet, to make them pick their feet up higher. Look showier."

"But how?"

"Ride them over coral. Use acid. There's a kind of yellow coral that stings if you touch it. Rub a piece of that into a horse's frog and his feet'll burn for hours."

Paulo paled at the idea. "But, Grandfather, is that allowed? Do very many men do that to their horses?"

"It's not allowed, but it's hard to prove. A few men do it. Not too many. But I've been beaten by sored horses."

"You wouldn't—"

"Of course not," Diego snapped. "A horse must move beautifully because he is proud, because he has fine breeding behind him, because he loves the man who rides him. Not because he is being tortured."

Paulo recalled the whole conversation with surprising clarity as he lay looking out the trailer window. His bed was in the shallow gooseneck part of the trailer that jutted forward over the truck. It had a curved green window at the front, through which he could see the long, lighted barn nearby. There were other barns beyond this one, and many other trailers and camping vehicles parked in a broad semicircle around them. Paulo lay on his stomach and watched the diminishing number of people going in and out of the barns, seeing to their horses.

Through his open trailer door he could hear an occasional whinny, a banging hoof against stall wall, the sudden high laughter of invisible girls.

A strange world, this new world of his, he mused. A life to which he was already unquestionably committed. The horses. The horses he knew and trusted and loved, but the people in this future of his—what were they going to be like? Did they love their horses as he did, or were they in it just to glorify themselves at the cost of their animals? Did people in this country rub yellow coral on their horses' feet to win blue ribbons?

Will I have to be like that someday? If I don't, will I be a failure in this profession? Am I even going to be a horse trainer, or what *do* I want?

Paulo's thoughts circled closer to here and now.

I know what I don't want. I don't want any damn stranger riding Danza in the show ring.

He rolled over on his back and braced one foot against the metal ceiling so close over his bed. A long, long sigh escaped him, but he didn't hear it.

The weeks of summer passed, and most were punctuated by a horse show trip. Sometimes it was just Paulo and the major, and Danza as their only entry. Sometimes Jan went along with Miel or Bobo, or both, depending on the size of the show and whether there were classes offered in which the mares might do well.

They became a practiced team at loading the trailer with the necessary tack, grooming tools, hay, grain, and bedding, and the cooler for soft drinks and the major's expensive beer.

This way of horse-showing began to seem familiar to Paulo, the long drives and overnight stays, the two-day shows at which the Paso Finos were just a small minority among more popular breeds.

Danza's placements in the Classic Fino classes were usually good. But never first. There were a substantial number of seconds and thirds, occasional lower placements, and occasionally no placement at all. By mid-July Danza had acquired the points necessary to qualify him for competition in the Paso Fino National Show in September. Other Paso Fino owners recognized Danza as a respected competitor and many expressed open admiration for the red-gold stallion.

But the blue ribbons continued to elude the major, and the man's hunger for them grew. He said little, but Paulo read the tension in the major's jaw muscles—the hard, flat look in the man's eyes when the competition was close and Danza emerged with the red instead of the maddeningly elusive blue ribbon.

Though his reasons differed from the major's, Paulo often came out of the ring frustrated with disappointment at Danza's placement. With his whole heart he knew that Danza was a wonderful horse, that he deserved better than he was getting. Every time another stallion was publicly designated superior to Danza, it was a stab wound to Paulo's loving pride in his horse, and to his pride in Diego Mendez, a pride Paulo had been unaware of until now.

It was Danza's weakened legs and feet that were keeping them from the wins, Paulo told himself continually. That was the only reason. Although the legs were gradually improving as the summer progressed, Danza still emerged from every show ring with a trembling in his legs that took hours to fade away. And the hooves were still too tender for contact with any but the softest earth and tanbark surfaces.

As the show season progressed and Paulo began to recognize the faces of his competitors, and to know which riders were private owners and which were professional trainers, he could not escape the fact that most of the top placements went to the professionals. From watching the afternoon classes Paulo knew this was less true in other divisions than it was in Classic Fino. The Pleasure and Versatility classes were often won by families like the Feldens who owned a small number of horses and showed them just for the fun of it. And the game classes, the egg-and-spoon races and water races, and the colorful costume classes, were frequently won by children. But the Fino Division was the supreme test of the Paso gait in its most intense form, and it demanded the utmost skill on the rider's part. The Fino Championship was the accolade of highest value to the serious breeder and the professional trainer.

Paulo refused to think that his own youth and lack of professional status might be the deciding factor between first and second place ribbons, for Danza. It wouldn't be right; it wouldn't be fair. He resolutely closed his mind to the thought, every time it came into his head.

It was a sweltering August afternoon. Paulo lay in a rope hammock that hung between his magnolia tree and a clothesline post. On a little folding table beside him were a Coke can, a stack of horse magazines, and an empty potato chip bag. Beneath the hammock the setter's speckled body lay in a shallow depression, bare earth she had dug up for its damp coolness.

The house behind Paulo was closed against the heat. The air-conditioner in the window droned and dripped. Inside, Paulo knew Janice would be sprawled before her afternoon soap operas and Dennis stretched out across his bed, snoring. Although the afternoons were not given the formal label of "siesta" at Paso Pines, the rhythm of the summer days was that of siesta. Work began early, before the gray dawns turned hot. It progressed until lunch, then slowed to a drowsy standstill while the weight of the sun-heated air pressed the breath and strength out of human and equine animals alike. By late afternoon the chores resumed and continued often until ten or eleven o'clock.

Paulo came up out of a drifting sleep and lifted the magazine from his chest. A good article on foaling problems, he'd been reading it with interest before his eyes had unfocused and closed.

He had just found his place on the page when he heard the major's car gliding out of the woods. Paulo glanced toward it, then looked again. Someone was with the major. The man stepped out of the car and Paulo recognized that he was a horseman. Something indefinable about the man's small, lean figure, the close-cropped salt-and-pepper hair, or maybe it was the no-nonsense look of the boots and jeans and polo shirt.

As the two men approached Paulo, he felt himself tighten. Instinctively he knew that this was no affable mare owner looking for a stud, no indulgent father shopping for a horse for his daughter. This man meant business, and even before the introductions, Paulo knew.

He tipped himself out of the hammock and pulled on his boots.

Major Kessler's eyes veered away from Paulo's. "Jordan, like you to meet my right-hand man, this is Paulo Camacho, from Puerto Rico. Paulo, Jordan Welch. Get Danza saddled up, will you? Jordan wants to take a look at him."

The trainer. The threat. He was here.

Paulo went through the familiar motions of putting Danza in the cross-ties in the spacious center aisle of the stable, of brushing his back and flanks and settling the good, darkly oiled saddle in place. He ducked under Danza's neck to let down the girth and off-side stirrup, ducked back again to tighten the girth.

All the time he kept his mind deliberately blank. But the man stood watching from the side of the aisle, with the major. His eyes assessed Danza's conformation, his quiet acceptance of the saddling procedure.

Paulo wanted to shout, to break the brittle silence of the three of them.

Major Kessler said, "Just ride him up and down the aisle here, a time or two, Paulo."

Paulo nodded and stepped up onto Danza. The aisle was floored with concrete, ideal for hearing and judging the rhythm of a horse's gait. Riding in here, Paulo was able to detect the slight flaw in Miel's fino. It was just a slight hesitation; one-two three-four, one-two three-four, when it should have been one-two-three-four, one-two-three-four. Like Danza's.

In spite of his apprehensions about this Jordan Welch fellow, Paulo couldn't resist gathering Danza into his fine, proud fino gait, and savoring the flawless cadence of it ringing on the concrete. Up the long aisle they went, then turned at the far door, without missing a beat, and back toward the men.

Paulo glanced at Mr. Welch. The stupid man was looking at Danza up high, at the horse's head and body, when he should have been studying the brio, the snapping action of Danza's feet, should be cocking his head to hear the beat.

"That's enough, Paulo," the major said. "Let's let Mr. Welch have a go at him."

Paulo did not want to slide down, to hand his horse to this man who obviously knew nothing about Paso Finos. But the major was watching him. Paulo got off and handed the reins to Major Kessler.

He defied in the only way he could think of. "Better not ride him in here any more. His feet can't take very much of that concrete."

"Right, Paulo. We'll go out to the ring. This way, Jordan." The major's hand dropped to Paulo's shoulder as they walked toward the ring, but Paulo stiffened under the touch, and the hand was dropped.

As Mr. Welch mounted Danza, then reached down expertly to lengthen the stirrup leathers, Paulo prayed for an explosion of wrath and wildness from Danza. A crazed stallion throwing himself over backward and mashing the life out of—well, at least injuring the enemy so he could never ride again.

But Danza stood as he always did, gathering himself for the excitement of motion, but waiting for his rider's signal.

Paulo wished for a bad performance. Sluggish fino. Breaking. Shying. Fighting the strange hand on his reins.

Danza started off somewhat less smoothly than with Paulo. But within half a circle of the ring Jordan Welch was settled into the feel of the horse and had Danza finoing smoothly.

"Got his hands too high," Paulo muttered. Then, reluctantly, "Who is he, major?"

The major hesitated, drew in a long breath, but spoke firmly. "He's a trainer, Paulo. If he likes Danza he's going to take him back to his stable for a few weeks, and show him at Lake Charles, and at the National."

Paulo's mind raced this way and that, away from the point of pain. "But can you do that without Grandfather's permission? Danza belongs to him, don't forget."

"Diego is the owner, but I am the lessee and as long as Danza is under lease to me, I'm in charge of his show career. And Paulo, don't forget, it's my money that is paying all of these show expenses, including several hundred dollars for Jordan Welch."

Paulo had no answer for that. He could only ache and rage silently. His hurt was not only at the loss of Danza to another rider; it was for the loss of something almost equally precious to Paulo, something inexpressible that the major was withholding. Withdrawing.

# *Eleven*

The Lake Charles Charity Horse Show was a large and glittering affair. Although it was barely past noon there was a feeling of evening formality about the arena. Stewards wore formal hunt attire, and trophy presenters held up long-skirted gowns as they tiptoed through the tanbark.

For Paulo, seated in a ringside box with the major and the Felden family, it was a crazy day. There was Danza two buildings away in his stall, being readied for the Classic Fino class, and Paulo was forbidden even to see him.

"It would just upset him," the major explained when they arrived. "Jordan said he's had a hard enough time getting Danza's mind off of you. If that horse saw you now it would undo all the work Jordan's put in on him these last weeks."

Paulo had accepted the edict, but not gracefully.

Only one more class, now. A Saddlebred fine harness class. Four elegant high-headed horses circled the ring at a majestic trot, drawing behind them gleaming carts in which gowned and fancy-hatted women drove with high-held reins.

Paulo didn't see them.

Beside him, Marilyn Felden said, "I bet you can hardly wait to see him, huh?"

Paulo made a tight little face, but said nothing.

"Boy, I'm sure glad my dad doesn't believe in hiring trainers. If he ever sent Nibs off someplace for some stranger to ride—"

Paulo turned on her. "What do you mean, he doesn't believe in trainers. He's the one who talked the major into hiring one. Well, one of the people anyway."

"Oh, that's different." Marilyn's round face grew unnaturally serious. "That's for people like him." She lowered her voice and slanted her eyes toward the major, who was talking in the other direction to Mrs. Felden. "People like the major are mainly in it for winning. In horses, I mean. Oh, they like their horses, maybe even love them, but not the same way we do, and you do, I think. If their horse can't win, they don't care about it anymore. Now me, and my family, we go to the shows mainly for fun. Our horses are our pets. I'd never sell Nibs, no matter what."

Paulo looked into that round, earnest face, and felt suddenly less alone.

The loudspeaker's music changed from Viennese to Spanish.

"Here they come," Paulo and Marilyn said together.

Danza was the first horse in the ring. Five others followed, but Paulo didn't see them. Three weeks without Danza, and Paulo was starved for the sight of him, the touch of him. His knees felt the curve of Danza's barrel between them; his hands lifted to the touch of Danza's mouth against the reins.

At first it was enough just to absorb the sight of that gleaming red body glinting gold in the highlights and fringed by a lengthening flow of black mane and tail. Black-booted legs, polished black hooves . . .

Paulo sat forward suddenly and stared at those legs, those hooves.

"He's not moving right," he said to the major.

Major Kessler, too, leaned forward and squinted as Danza danced by. "Looks all right to me. In fact, I like the way he's moving. Got more spirit than . . . before."

"Than when I was riding him?"

But the argument died as Paulo and the major turned their attention fully on Danza.

Paulo spoke only to himself now. He's picking his feet up too high. He's prancing like a darned Saddlebred or something. That's not how a Paso is supposed to move. Don't these fools know that? Not a high prance. Quick snap at the pasterns, but keep the feet low to the ground. That's not right, what he's got Danza doing out there. What is he doing to my horse?

For a moment Paulo took his eyes away from Danza's feet and looked at the rest of the horse. Good weight, beautiful shine to his coat, but his ears were flattened, and every few steps Danza's tail made an angry wringing motion. As the horse came close again Paulo could see anger and . . . something else . . . in Danza's eyes. Pain? Was it pain?

The six stallions lined up, and the judge sent his message to the announcer.

"First place in Classic Fino, Stallions, is Danza, owned by Diego Mendez, ridden by Jordan Welch. Second place—"

"Hooeee!" Major Kessler shouted, and banged Paulo's back. "Finally did it! He won his class. See, Paulo, it takes that little extra touch that only a professional can give a horse. I was right to send him to Welch. Now we have a real shot at the National Championship next week. Hooeee, we're on the right track now."

Paulo stood up. "I want to go see him."

"No." The major's voice was flat. "He'll be going back into the Championship class later on. And frankly, Paulo, Jordan doesn't want Danza to see you at all. Said it would just upset the horse, and with the National show next weekend, let's not take a chance. He's the trainer, after all. I'm paying him for his expertise, and I intend to follow his advice."

Paulo stared down at the man. "You mean I can't see him at all? We drove all this way down here just to sit in the audience and—"

"Now, son . . ."

"I'm not your son," he flared, and ran from the box.

Paulo was out of the building and halfway to the barns when he heard Marilyn's voice. "Hey, wait up."

He stopped. A friend suddenly seemed just what he needed.

"What are you going to do?" Sweat trickled down her face from the running, and her eyes were warm with concern.

"See my horse."

She fell into step beside him.

But Jordan Welch met them in the aisle of the barn. Paulo asked politely, then tried to reason, then shouted in anger he could no longer hide. The man was adamant.

Paulo and Marilyn turned and went outside, but lingered at the edge of the door. When Paulo looked back down the aisle he saw Jordan Welch talking to a uniformed security guard, motioning to Danza's stall and to Paulo.

"Come on," Marilyn said, "let's go get something to eat. That guard isn't going to let you near Danza."

"But he's my horse."

"Yeah, but whose word do you think that guard would take, yours or old Welch's?"

Paulo caved in under her logic. He wasn't interested in food, but he followed Marilyn to the lunch stand to escape the tantalizing nearness of Danza. And to avoid being alone.

A thought, like a prick of pain, refused to be banished or ignored. The major. A firm word from the major and Paulo would be allowed to go to Danza. "Doesn't he know how bad I want to see my horse? Or aren't I important to him at all? I told him something was wrong with Danza, the way he was moving in that ring, but he didn't take my word for it. Or else he didn't care."

The lunchroom was a sprawling place with tables across one end where aproned women sold hot dogs and barbeques. Long tables filled most of the room. The main lunch rush was past, leaving empty paper cups and crumpled sandwich papers scattered over the tabletops. Paulo sat down sideways to a table, his feet on the next chair, his shoulders hunched against all his miseries, while Marilyn went for her food.

Two men stepped past him and sat behind Paulo at the next table. He glanced at them only long enough to catalog them, by their riding clothes, as Tennessee Walker people. Paulo had found mild amusement in the variety of show clothes these Americans wore. A distinct outfit for each kind of horse. Skinny, hipless girls in high black boots and pale breeches and velvet caps, those were hunters or hunt seat riders. Long-jacketed suits and little derby hats, Saddlebred people. For Walking Horses a similar outfit with subtle differences. For Quarter horses and Appaloosas, cowboy hats and fancy shirts and fringed suede chaps. And the Paso people in their dark Spanish-formal suits and ruffled shirts and flat-brimmed hats.

". . . Jordan Welch gone to Paso Finos now, I see."

The voice jerked at Paulo's attention. One of the men behind him. He sat rigid, listening.

"You're kidding," the other man said. "What's he want with a camel-shuffler?"

Paulo's eyes bulged with compressed anger.

"Got to make a living, I guess. He pretty well blew himself out of the water with the Walking Horse people, and I doubt he could get anything good in Saddlebreds now. Pasos might not be such a bad move for him, considering. Looked like a pretty decent horse he had. Won his class with him, I believe. I saw him coming out a while ago."

Marilyn approached, chattering. Paulo waved her silent, and motioned with his head toward the men, whose backs were toward Paulo.

146

One of them spoke, and Paulo strained to hear. "How'd you do last weekend? Were you at Mobile?"

Marilyn looked puzzled. She held her dripping chili dog aloft, waiting.

Abruptly Paulo swung around and tapped the nearer man on the arm. "Pardon me for interrupting. I heard you talking about Jordan Welch. What did he do to blow himself out of the water with Walking Horse people?" Paulo wasn't sure what the term meant, but his voice was as firm as if he did.

The men glanced at one another in a guarded way. "Why do you ask?"

"Because that camel-shuffler he's riding belongs to me. My grandfather. And I don't like the way he's treating him."

This time the exchanged glance between the men was one of doubt bordering on amusement. Paulo felt very young and very foreign and not at all like the owner of an expensive show horse.

The near man said, "If the horse belongs to you, then what's the problem? Fire Welch."

Suddenly it became vital for Paulo to know what these men knew about Welch. Armed with that information he could attack the major and convince him to get Danza away from that man. He was almost sure that the look he'd seen in Danza's eyes had been one of pain, and he could see that look clearly now. He scooted his chair around and hunched forward, his eyes burning.

"Look, it's true. Danza belongs to my grandfather, down in Puerto Rico, but he's always been my horse, to raise and train and ride. He got foundered and my

147

grandfather couldn't take care of him good enough, so he loaned him to Major Kessler to bring up here where the vets are better. Major Kessler was just supposed to use him for one season of breeding and then send him back home, and me too. Only now he's started showing him and charging other people lots of money to breed their mares to him. And I wasn't winning enough with Danza, so he sent him away to Jordan Welch, and Danza was hurting. In the ring. I saw his eyes, and something was hurting him, but Mr. Welch won't let me in the barn so I can't see for myself."

This time when the men exchanged looks, there was acceptance of Paulo's story, and compassion.

The near man cleared his throat. "Well, we really don't know the facts of the situation. It's just stable gossip but, for what it's worth, maybe you have the right to hear it. Welch used to be a pretty successful trainer in Tennessee Walking Horses. Got a nice stable down around New Orleans, I think. Did a lot of winning, but he was in and out of trouble with the authorities all the time, for soring."

"Soring—" It all came clear in Paulo's mind. Danza's unusually high steps, the wringing tail, the look of pain in his eyes.

"Yes. Well, everybody does it, you understand. Only some people are more blatant about it than others. But what finally cooked it for Welch was, he sored a client's horse so badly that the horse was crippled for life. That happens from time to time, too, unfortunately, but in this case the owner was quite influential in the breed, and the horse was a special favorite of his. Just a young animal, lots of potential. The owner said

Welch would never work in Walkers again, and I guess it wasn't an empty threat."

Crippled for life. Paulo sat back and let the horrible possibilities wash over him. A whole year of working and hoping and massaging, of caring for Danza when he was a blue-gray hairless pile of bones with no feet, of massaging wasted leg muscles until Paulo's own muscles ached unbearably, rejoicing over that first rim of new hoof emerging from Danza's coronets— Was it all for this? The weeks and months of pampering those foundered feet so that no gravel, no concrete brought back the agony that Danza had borne longer than any innocent animal should have to bear anything . . . and now this stupid, criminal gringo was deliberately hurting those feet so the major could get his blue ribbon and Welch could make a living.

Marilyn ignored Paulo's sickened silence. She scooted her chair closer to the conversation and said, "But why do you people do that to your horses? How can you love horses and deliberately hurt them?"

The near man shook his head. "Believe me, honey, we don't like it. We do it because we have to. As long as everyone else is doing it, we have to or we simply won't be in the ribbons. I have hundreds of thousands of dollars wrapped up in my stock and my stable facilities, and I've got to be able to sell horses at substantial prices or I can't afford to stay in the business. And you have to have the show wins. And to win, your horse has got to do the big lick. It's as simple as that."

"But isn't it illegal or something?" Marilyn cried.

"Oh, yes. Certainly it's illegal. The Horse Protection Act passed in 1970, federal law. Didn't do a bit of good. Not enough money to enforce it. And when the inspectors find out how to detect one kind of soring, the trainers come up with another, more sophisticated. First it was oil of mustard. Caused terribly bloody blisters around a horse's coronets, under their boots. Bichloride of mercury was another one."

Marilyn's face flushed with emotion, but she said in an even voice, "Well, I'm sorry for your horses. And I'm just glad we don't have it in our breed."

Both men laughed, and one said, "Don't kid yourself, kid. Every breed has its secrets. Dilated eyes in Arabians, tranquilizers in Quarter horses, drug stimulants in Saddlebreds, and plenty more that I don't know about, I'm sure. It's in every breed at least to some degree—maybe just at the top levels of competition, but it's there."

Paulo muttered, "Americanos," and the near man turned on him. "It's in every country, too, kid. You don't need to be so holy. Down there you use yellow coral. Other things too, probably, but I've heard of that one."

He couldn't sit still any longer. Leaving Marilyn to end the conversation politely, he ran out of the building. Major Kessler was walking toward him.

Paulo dodged a hackney pony and cart, and ran to the major.

"Paulo, there you are. I was looking for you. Come on back to the box. The Fino Championship is after this next class. You don't want to miss that."

"I have to talk to you," Paulo panted. "We have to get Danza away from that man. He's hurting him."

150

"What? You don't know what you're talking about—"

A clot of laughing teenagers swarmed between them.

"Listen, major, I was just talking to these men in the lunchroom . . ."

The major took Paulo's arm and started him toward the show building. "This is no place to talk about it, and we don't want to miss Danza's class."

His voice was firm, almost as though he didn't want to hear what Paulo was going to say, Paulo thought.

Marilyn caught up with them, and the three of them climbed the steps to their box just as the Fino Championship class was entering the ring.

Paulo watched, in spite of his anguish. It was too late now to get Danza out of the class, anyway.

Six horses entered the ring, necks arched, long manes billowing, Danza and the second-place horse from the stallion class, then the first- and second-place winners from the gelding and mare classes. Again Danza moved with unnaturally high lifting of his feet, with the angry lashing of his tail.

"See," Paulo shook the major's elbow, "can't you see how he's moving?"

"He's moving like a winner, Paulo. Now, please keep your voice down." The major glanced toward Marilyn and her parents in the seats behind him and Paulo.

Paulo lowered his voice, but tried once again. "These men in the lunchroom, they know Mr. Welch, major. They were telling me he used to put things on Walking Horses' hooves to make them sore, so they'd win, and he made one horse permanently crippled and got into lots of trouble over it, and that's why he's trying to get into Paso Finos now. And I know he's doing it to Danza. You have to stop him."

"Doing what?" The major appeared to be only half-listening as he watched Danza, narrow-eyed.

"Putting mustard on his feet," Paulo shouted.

Several people turned to look at him, some grinning.

The major laughed openly.

Paulo grew red with fury, but lowered his voice again. "Something like mustard. Something that burns their feet and makes awful blisters. That's why Danza is picking up his feet so high. It's hurting him. Please, major. Take him away from Mr. Welch."

The man laid a restraining hand on Paulo's knee. "Shhh. We'll talk about it later. I want to watch this."

The judge sent his message to the announcer, and the loudspeaker crackled, "Grand Champion, Fino Division, Danza, owned by—"

Paulo's heart sank.

As the major rose to leave the box, Paulo said, "Look at his feet yourself, if you don't believe me. Or make Mr. Welch let me see him. You're the one who hired him. He'll have to let you see Danza."

The major turned swiftly on Paulo and said in a low hard voice, "Now, you listen to me. I am paying Mr. Welch to use his expertise to get wins with Danza. You rode the horse all summer and never did better than second place. One time out, and Welch has won a Championship class with him. I am not going to insult the man by questioning his methods, and if he feels it would be bad for Danza for you to see him, then that's it. His word is final. As long as he can get results like this out of that horse, neither you nor I will interfere. Is that understood?"

"But he's hurting him," Paulo wailed.

The major was already down the steps and away to collect his rosette and trophy.

It was nearly midnight. Paulo lay on his bed in the motel room, staring at the television screen as though he were watching the movie. Except for the silvery light from the screen, the room was dark. It was a nice room, assembly line plush, a major motor hotel chain, with velvety wallpaper and pictures that looked like real art.

The major's bed, next to Paulo's, was still smoothly made. The major was out somewhere having dinner and drinks with Mr. Welch and some of the other Paso people. This time Paulo had not been invited, and he was glad, he told himself.

Restlessness grew in him, a need to do something. Finally he flung himself off the bed and pushed his feet into his loafers. He smacked the on-off knob on the television, grabbed his room key, and fled down the long blue and green hallway and out the thick glass door at the end.

Outside, the highway stretched away toward the show grounds six, seven blocks away. Paulo started at an easy lope. As he ran he thought, How am I going to get in? The entrance will be guarded, for sure. And a Puerto Rican kid in old jeans and t-shirt, this time of the night, no way they're going to let me in. Over a fence, maybe, around at the back of the grounds. And if I can get in the barn, what then? Just see him? See his feet?

Just see him.

The ache in Paulo's chest had nothing to do with running.

# Twelve

The way in was easier than Paulo had expected, a side road, a gate that was padlocked but simple to climb over, and a barn still open and lighted at the far end where a knot of people were standing around a stall in the Saddlebred area, drinking and laughing.

Three aisles away in the row of Paso Fino stalls, the barn was dim and empty of people except for a young man in a sleeping bag in a vacant stall. A few horses shuffled and whickered at Paulo as he peered into stall after stall.

He heard Danza's soft snort from three stalls away. The dark shape of Danza's head appeared over the stall door, straining toward him.

"There's my boy," Paulo whispered. In his excitement he almost forgot to be quiet in opening the stall door.

"Danza."

Paulo wrapped his arms around the horse's neck and buried his face in the long, coarse strands of Danza's mane; the horse turned his head so far around that Paulo was enclosed in the bend of Danza's neck.

What have they been doing to you? Paulo wanted to

155

ask. More strongly than ever before in his life, he wished for the ability to read Danza's thoughts, to communicate his own to the mind within that broad, flat skull.

The light within the stall was too dim to see details, but Paulo leaned against Danza's shoulder and ran his hand down the black-stockinged leg. "Give me your foot," he whispered.

Danza tensed, and stood firm. Never before had he refused to lift a foot, even during the painful months of his illness. Paulo's fingers probed gently around the pastern, around the rim of the coronet. Heat. A puffy tenderness, like blisters. Danza snorted and shied away from Paulo's touch.

Paulo needed no bright lights to complete his examination.

For a long time he stood stroking Danza . . . thinking. Then, afraid of being seen, he sat down in a corner of the stall, elbows on his knees, hands dangling.

Think, think, think, he told himself. Got to get Danza away from that man. Got to do it now. First thing in the morning he's going to load him up and truck him back to his stable unless I stop him. How? Get him out of here. I could take him now. Probably nobody would stop me in the barn. But I couldn't get him through the gate. The guy at the gate would never believe he was my horse. They'd arrest me for horse-stealing.

And even if I could get him off the grounds, what would I do with him then? Can't ride him all the way to Puerto Rico. I don't know anybody here in Lake Charles. Nowhere to take him.

At the mental picture of himself kidnapping Danza, Paulo grew suddenly fierce.

Why should I have to sneak out of here like a thief with him? Danza is more mine than the major's. I have a right to protect him from being hurt. And after everything I went through to see that he has feet, I have a better right than anybody else to make sure nobody hurts him anymore. I hurt him in the first place by not being careful of that latch rope, but that's a whole lot different from putting acid or whatever on him and deliberately hurting him to get blue ribbons. He's my horse, and nobody does that to my horse.

After a while, with no real plan of action except to hold firm and demand justice, Paulo relaxed and dozed, his head back against the stall wall. Danza stood over him, his chin just above the boy's hair. For the first time in weeks, the little red stallion felt that his world was right.

"What in hell are you doing in there?" Welch shouted.

The morning sun was well up. Paulo had been awake for some time, waiting, rehearsing. He stood and brushed the wood shavings from his seat.

"I'm staying with my horse," he said. It didn't come out sounding as strong as he had meant it to.

"That's what you think. Listen, kid, what's your name, Paul, I told you I didn't want you upsetting Danza, and I meant it." He turned and shouted, "Watchman!"

"You mean you didn't want me to see his feet. You hurt him, and I'm not going to let you do it anymore.

He belongs to my grandfather, and I am his agent in this country. You're fired."

Paulo almost smiled. That last part came out pretty good.

A uniformed watchman approached. Mr. Welch turned on him. "What kind of security do you people have in this place, anyway? This boy apparently got in here during the night. I want him out of here."

The guard moved to take Paulo's arm. Paulo stood his ground, but tightened the arm that lay across Danza's neck, as though to anchor himself.

He stood as straight as he could and said to the watchman, "This horse belongs to my family in Puerto Rico. Mr. Welch was just his trainer, but I fired him."

The watchman hesitated, looked at Mr. Welch. A few people stopped in the aisle to watch and listen and glance curiously at one another.

"Is that right?" the watchman asked Mr. Welch.

The man looked suddenly defensive. "His grandfather is the official owner of the horse, yes, but I was hired by a Major Kessler who has the horse in this country on lease. He's the man who's paying me, and no little snot like this is going to stand there and tell me he's firing me."

Marilyn Felden's face appeared suddenly around the stall door.

Paulo said, "Marilyn! Go get the major. And your dad," he added as an afterthought. He felt cornered, overpowered by the authorities around him, and instinctively he wanted Mr. Felden's calm fair-mindedness.

Suddenly the major appeared. "Paulo, where on

earth have you been all night? I was just about to—
what's going on here?"

Paulo looked at him, and old emotions rose to clog
his throat. This man, this good, kind, strong man who
was the first to accord Paulo Camacho the dignity of
respect—was he still there behind that familiar long
freckled face? Was there any love? Was it all the hungry imaginings of his own need?

Dark eyes locked on pale ones. "Major, he has been
blistering Danza's feet. I had to come and see for myself, and he has. Look. Come here and look." He
picked up Danza's near hoof and touched the horny
frog area. Danza jerked away.

The major looked, but from a distance. "Paulo, this
is nothing to make a scene about. We'll talk about it
later—"

"No." As Paulo spoke he felt the pain of betrayal.
There was no time to probe it now, but it was there
behind the urgency of the moment. "Danza is mine,
and I'm taking him away from you. From both of you.
I'm taking him home."

The crowd in the aisle was large by now. With a
wash of relief Paulo saw Mr. Felden near the stall
door. Paulo turned toward the crowd and raised his
voice. "All you people out there. He's been soring my
horse and I don't want him to. Can't somebody help?"

There was an uneasy silence, as though no one knew
what action to take, what words to say.

Suddenly Mr. Felden said, "Paulo, if there's anything I can do, if you need transportation or a place
to keep Danza or anything like that, you can count
on me."

The offer dazzled Paulo. The way out . . .

"What's the trouble here?" A new voice, a new face, an official from the show committee came through the crowd with the ease of authority.

The major said, "It's nothing, sir. We can handle it."

A woman in the crowd said, "The boy's made an accusation of soring, Mr. Kenney. I think you ought to look into it."

"Says it's his horse," another voice called.

And a lower mutter, "Jordan Welch. Isn't he the one that—"

"Some to-do about a Walking Horse, year or so ago, I remember that. At it again, looks like."

Mr. Kenney announced, "All right, folks, we'll take care of it. Now," in a lower tone, "Major Kessler, Mr. Welch, and you, young man, let's go over to the office where we can talk about this in private. We'll have the show vet examine the horse, and we'll take it from there."

In a small office behind the lunchroom they sat in a tense ring, Major Kessler, Jordan Welch, Mr. Felden —no one so far had objected to his presence, and Paulo was grateful to have him there—and Paulo himself. Mr. Kenney leaned back in his chair behind a cluttered desk, and drummed on the desk with his pen.

He heard them out, then looked up as the show veterinarian came in and handed him a paper. "Sored, all right, no question about that," the man said, and left.

Mr. Kenney sighed. "I'm not sure just what authority the show committee has in a situation like this. Ordinarily a complaint about soring comes from a competitor, not from the owner. Or, in this case, the owner's grandson." He glanced at Paulo, then at the major.

"Is there any dispute here about the ownership of the horse?"

Paulo shook his head. The major said, "I have only a verbal agreement with Mr. Mendez about the terms of the lease, as I already explained. It's up to Mr. Mendez to say when he wants the horse returned to Puerto Rico. There's no problem there."

Mr. Kenney looked at Jordan Welch. "Welch, we've been through this before with you. Whatever disciplinary action the American Horse Show Association may want to take is up to them. Your horse will forfeit his wins at this show, of course, and if I may say so, it's a shame. I saw him in action; he's a fine animal and very probably would have won fairly if he'd been allowed to do so.

"Now, it's up to you people to work out your internal differences. If this young man wants to take the horse with him when he leaves here, and if he has the means of doing so, the show committee will allow that. Now, I'm needed over at the announcer's booth. You folks can stay and use the office if you'd like."

He nodded to them all, and left.

The room grew still and the atmosphere strained. Paulo ached to grab Danza and get out of here, away from Welch, and especially away from the major. He could hardly bear to look at the major for the flood of memories that threatened to smother him. The smiles, the words of praise, the major's arm dropped casually across his shoulder in a gesture that had the power to warm Paulo and expand him to man-size.

"How could you do it to Danza?" Paulo flared, startling even himself. "After all that horse went through, all the pain in his feet from the foundering. I worked so hard to get him better, and every day you came out to the stable to see how he was, just like you really cared about him. And now you hire this—this *asesino* to hurt Danza just so he wins better for you. Well, you aren't a good man, major. You aren't good enough to have my horse. Or my respect." Paulo finished on a note of triumph at the way his words sounded.

"Paulo, look, I didn't mean for it to turn out—" The major hesitated.

Mr. Welch stood up. "I don't have time to sit around in here all day. What's it going to be, major? Do I take the horse with me, or what?"

Major Kessler floundered. It occurred to Paulo that he and the major had driven down in the car. There was no way to transport Danza back to Paso Pines.

Mr. Felden cleared his throat. Paulo whirled to him. "Will you take me and Danza home with you? I'll call my grandfather and get the money to ship Danza home as quick as I can. Please. I don't want him to go back with Mr. Welch."

The major said, "Now, Paulie, there's no need for that. You come on home with me for now, and Jordan can take Danza back to his stable, just to board until we get this all settled. And don't forget the National next week. Danza is qualified and entered, and we want—"

"No." Paulo's voice cracked under the heat of his emotions.

162

Mr. Felden said, "We have room in our trailer, Paulo. You and Danza are welcome to come home with us for as long as necessary. For that matter, you could go to the National with us if you should decide to show him. We're only taking Nibs."

Paulo nodded. This kindness robbed him of his voice.

Mr. Felden stood up. "You know where our trailer is. You come along whenever you're ready. Major, I hope this won't cause undue hard feelings. I know I'm probably butting into something that isn't my concern. But, dammit, I've seen what this business of soring horses, drugging them, injuring them in all sorts of ways—I've seen the harm it's done in other breeds, not only to the horses but to the people, to the spirit of the sport. I fell in love with Paso Finos because they are such fine creatures naturally. Naturally, major. When they collect themselves and move like poetry it's because they feel beautiful, not because they're in pain.

"I've got children at home, major, and thank God they are all animal lovers. My wife and I have taught them always to be thoughtful of their pets and to treat them with love. What kind of parents would we be if we began torturing our horses, or allowing our kids to do so, for any reason at all, but especially if we were doing it just to gain an unfair advantage in the show ring. I'll tell you something, major, I'd sell my horses first, and I love those nags of mine just about as much as I do my wife and kids. And if I can do one little thing, like helping Paulo out right now, to help stop the practice of soring before it gets started in our breed, then by God I'm going to do it."

He left, and Jordan Welch slipped out after him.

The air in the office seemed charged with electricity.

"Well, Paulo."

Paulo stood stiff and silent.

The major said, "Jan and Dennis will be awfully sorry to lose you."

And you? Paulo cried silently.

"I'll have Janice pack up your things and send them on to you."

Another silence.

"Paulo, I'm sorry."

"Me, too."

But it was not words or actions for which Paulo was sorry. If he had been able at that moment to sort out all of the miseries that rose in him, all the minor sorries would have fallen away from the one central regret— that of having loved someone he could not respect.

# *Thirteen*

Paulo sat on Danza, bareback, while the horse cropped at the front lawn. His hand stroked Danza's neck, but his eyes were on the road, where the mailman's car would be appearing any minute now. Bringing the money.

It was Wednesday. Three days now since he and Danza had come to New Orleans, to this house, this family. Three days since his mother's voice over the phone had said, "I'll tell your Grandfather just as soon as he gets home, Paulo. Don't worry. You go ahead and make the arrangements for shipping Danza, and we'll send the money just as soon as we can, for both of you to come home."

Wednesday. No word yet. And no decision about the National. Day after tomorrow Mr. Felden and Marilyn and Nibs would be leaving for Georgia for the Paso Fino National Championship Show, with or without Paulo and Danza. And still Paulo could come to no decision. The Feldens' veterinarian had given Paulo a salve for Danza's blistered areas. The salve and three days of luxurious rest in a deeply bedded stall had all but removed the tenderness in Danza's feet. Probably by Saturday, Paulo told himself, Danza would be healed enough for the show ring. But until he heard something from Diego Paulo felt up in the air, unable to do anything but drift through the waiting time.

It was a good place to wait. The family was warm as a litter of pups, and indignant about Danza's blistered feet. The young children competed for Paulo's attention as they brought their belongings and accomplishments to him, to show him. Marilyn was his friend, and the elder Feldens accepted him as another of their children as easily as they would have accepted a neighbor child coming to spend the night.

Even the house and stable seemed comfortable to Paulo, whose natural tendency was to clench up in strange places. It was a rambling Spanish-style house in a neighborhood of others similarly built, with an orange tile roof and arched porticos and dagger plants in pots along the drive. The lawn was attractively planned, but scarred by hoofprints and the collie's recreational digging. Bicycles leaned against trees and portico pillars.

The stable was a delight to Paulo. It, too, was Spanish in design but purely American in equine comfort. The center aisle was broad and bright. Along one side were three large stalls, each with a back door leading onto the small pasture. Across the aisle was one extra-roomy stall, which was given to Danza, a tack room where each halter and bucket had its hook, and an open area where the collie slept with cats curled beside him and where youngsters sat on hay bales to watch the grooming, to chatter, or just to be near the horses.

Each of the family's three horses had its name hand-painted by Marilyn on its stall door. The lettering was childish but decorated with improbable-looking flowers that showed the artist's love if not her artistic realism. Ceiling fans kept the stable comfortably cool and helped defeat the flies.

Paulo had spent most of these last days with Danza, just being with him, feeling the strands of their closeness reknitting. But during the afternoon hours, when Marilyn and the other children were home from school, the three Felden horses were saddled and everyone rode.

Paulo, as honored guest, was given the use of Noche, while Marilyn and one small brother rode the gray mare, Nibs, and two other children, sometimes three, rode Carmelita, a light chestnut mare who theoretically belonged to Mrs. Felden, as Noche belonged to Mr. Felden. Noche was a rangy black gelding, large for a Paso Fino and somewhat rough in his gaits, but good-natured and willing.

The three horses and their several riders set out each afternoon along the blacktopped road that wound among semi-suburban acreages. Some of the homes along the road were more expensive-looking than the Feldens', some less, but most had small stables, small pastures fenced in with white planks or rustic cedar poles. A mile down the road was a park threaded with bridle paths that led among live oaks fantastically bearded with Spanish moss.

It was a pleasant time for Paulo, and yet he felt suspended between two realities: his life at Paso Pines with Janice and Dennis and the horses and the major, and the journey that lay in the immediate future, the boat trip with Danza back to Puerto Rico. Home.

167

And between now and then—what? Georgia and the National? Problems? Not enough money coming from Diego for the shipping costs and his own fare? Diego saying, "Let him find his own way home; he wanted to go to America so bad, let him earn his own way home."

Danza and Paulo looked up, together, as the mailman's car drove into the turnaround and pulled up beside the mailbox. Paulo slipped to the ground and took the bundle of envelopes and magazines. He barely heard the man's cheerful comment on the weather.

No envelope from Puerto Rico.

Nothing.

Paulo started toward the stable, so depressed that he forgot he had the family's mail in his hand. Danza plodded after him.

From within the house came the ring of the telephone. A moment later Mrs. Felden came banging out through the kitchen door.

"Paulo!"

He closed Danza's stall door and turned toward the house.

"I've got it," he said, holding up the mail.

She came across the yard looking not much older than Marilyn. She was grinning broadly. "Paulo, guess who that was on the phone. Your grandfather! He's at the airport, wanted to know how to get here. Come on, hop in."

Paulo froze. Grandfather, here? In person? Disbelief gave way to a warm, spreading joy as Paulo pictured the solid figure of Diego, the figure that had dominated his whole life. Diego was often a silent force, pushing the boy to his best efforts by the withholding of praise rather than by the giving of it, but always it was Diego whom Paulo strove to please. And those feelings were still there, Paulo realized now. A year in America had only hidden them beneath a blanket of new experiences.

It was for Diego as much as for Danza that Paulo had been fighting, first the founder and then the ceaseless showring battles.

For Diego. And now he was here.

With equally balanced eagerness and trepidation Paulo walked with Mrs. Felden through the lounge area of the New Orleans airport. All the way to the airport he'd been remembering his hurried leavetaking from home a year before, remembering Diego's absence during those last harried hours.

But Paulo's awareness of other people had been stretched and exercised, this past year. There were complex emotions at work beneath the surface of everyone around him. He was beginning to comprehend that now; the major had taught him that, if nothing else.

Grandfather never did say much, Paulo thought, especially about the things that mattered most to him. So maybe he cared more about me than I thought. Maybe that's why he came here instead of just sending the money to ship Danza home. Maybe because of me. Or maybe not. It might just be the horse. Oh well. I'm *glad* he's here.

And there he was, striding through the crowd, an

erect, square figure in an old-fashioned shiny black suit, his white hair and beard framing the strong, leathery face.

"Grandfather." Paulo ran the last few steps, then stood awkwardly before the man, not knowing what to do with his arms.

Diego stared down into the boy's face for a long silent moment, then the sharpness melted from his eyes and he held Paulo close against his chest.

"You've grown, boy."

Paulo could only nod.

Diego released him. "Let's go see Danza."

They made a sizable group on the patio—the six Feldens scattered over chairs, grass, and a picnic table that held the remnants of supper, Paulo and Diego, Danza and Nibs grazing at the ends of their reins, and the collie sprawled over the remaining space. Danza wore a borrowed saddle; Diego had ridden him about the yard with an expression of intense, inward-turning joy on his leathery face. Nibs wore only the marks of three sets of sweaty legs ranging down the length of her back.

In spite of the letters and occasional snapshots Paulo had sent, over the year, Diego had not been prepared for the sight of Danza.

Not only had the blue-gray, footless, hairless monstrosity vanished, he had been replaced by a stallion of greater majesty than even Diego's early optimism had foreseen for the colt. Danza's head at maturity was a study in balance, in fine breeding, and in glowing intelligence. The neck, on the side not hidden by the luxurious new mane, was clean and fine at the throatlatch but swelling now with the muscled crest of a mature stallion. The copper-colored body was sleek, dappled, as short-coupled as Bonanza's but with a smoother finish of muscling over the croup. His legs were clean and straight, his pasterns long. The tail that completed the picture was a black cascade. In another few months it would sweep the ground.

Diego had made satisfactorily warm comments on Nibs, had assured the Felden children that the foal she carried, sired by Danza, would be magnificent. He had patted the mare, but his eyes went back again and again to the stallion grazing in the flower border at the patio's edge.

It was nearly dark. Mrs. Felden carried supper dishes into the house and came back with a tray of drinks.

Diego accepted his. "I owe you a great debt for helping my grandson, and Danza. If your mare was not already bred to Danza, I would offer you a free breeding as a token of gratitude."

"We have another mare," the youngest child piped. Mrs. Felden shushed her, embarrassed.

"No thanks needed," Mr. Felden said. "We've enjoyed having them here. Paulo's like another one of our own, and a horse like Danza, well, it's an honor to have him in our stable even for a few days."

The little girl piped, "It's an honor to shovel his manure. I've been helping Paulo, haven't I, Paulo?"

Paulo grabbed her foot and shook it, as gentle laughter blew on the night air.

Mr. Felden said, "We have to make a decision here,

though, about this trip to Georgia. Now, there's no reason why we can't all go, including Danza and Paulo and you, Mr. Mendez. Margaret will be bringing the car, so there'll be room for passengers. We can do a little shifting with our motel reservations, that should be no trouble. And the horse has qualified, after all. It's an honor just to qualify for the Championship show, and Danza has earned it. But it's up to you."

Diego looked at Paulo.

"I think his feet will be okay, Grandfather."

Diego was silent, pondering. Finally he said, "All right. I would like to see your National show. We can take Danza, and if his feet are bothering him, we will withdraw his entry. Do you agree to that, Paulo?"

Paulo nodded.

After a while the Feldens gathered themselves and went into the house, obedient to eye-signals from Mrs. Felden, who sensed that Paulo and Diego needed time alone. Marilyn put Nibs away, then ran to join them, veering at the last minute to give Diego a hug and a smack on the cheek that startled the old man and sent a flush of pleasure up his neck.

Night insects became suddenly loud in the absence of voices.

Paulo lapsed into Spanish. "I was getting worried when the money didn't come. I was afraid you might not want to send it."

"Not want to?"

"Well, I know you didn't like it very much when I came here."

"No. I didn't like it, Pablo. I lost too many of my

sons to this place. You were . . . too important to me. I didn't want you to come. But it was right, what you did."

"Then you weren't mad at me all this time?"

Diego was silent for a moment. He was not yet accustomed to this young man who had been little Paulo. There were elements of man in the boy now, that had not been there before. And Diego knew, with a quiet, swelling joy, that Paulo was going to be his, as none of his other sons or grandsons had been. Paulo was a horseman. And Paulo was a Puerto Rican to the marrow of his bones, in spite of a year of exposure to life as an American. There was no mistaking the boy's eagerness for home. At last, Diego thought, I have my son.

"Were you mad at me?" Paulo insisted. "You didn't say goodbye when I left, or answer my letters."

Diego sighed. It was not easy for him to talk about his feelings.

"No, Paulo. Not mad. I was afraid."

"Of what?" To Paulo the idea of Diego Mendez fearing anything was surprising, and oddly reassuring.

The old man looked away. "Losing you."

There was nothing to say. Insects chirred. Television noises came faintly from a back bedroom.

Paulo said, "You brought the money? For shipping Danza home?"

"Yes."

"How did you get it?"

There was no answer. Paulo glanced toward the old

man and saw a shimmering in his eyes reflected from the yard light.

"How did you get the money, Grandfather?"

"It's not important."

"Yes, it is."

"I sold Bonanza."

# *Fourteen*

The Blue Ridge Horse Park was just that—a park of great natural beauty, dedicated to every aspect of equine sport. It lay in a broad, flat valley, high enough in the mountain range to offer a panorama of soft blue-green hills folding and fading in all directions.

Around a small natural lake ranged racetracks, show rings, acres of bridle paths, and an Olympic-quality cross-country course. In an elegant brick stable one sample horse from every breed known to America lived, on display, so that visitors could stroll through and see a Trachener, a Fjord Horse, a Paso Fino, a Connemara Pony, as well as the more common breeds.

Diego made few comments as he and Paulo walked around the park, but Paulo sensed his wonder and pleasure. When they emerged from the Horses of America stable where the various breeds were displayed, Diego said, "It's good for us to see so many other kinds of horses, Pablo. We live on our little island with our Pasos, and we forget that it's not the whole world."

But Paulo's mind couldn't stay long away from Danza.

"Let's start back," he said. "It's almost ten. They'll be starting the Weanling Bella Forma classes pretty soon."

He and Diego began angling back toward the area that was, for this weekend, taken over by the Paso Fino people—a fine old brick stable and, nearby, a grass show ring contained by a neatly trimmed hedge. Banners, a trophy table loaded with silver, and Spanish music from the loudspeaker all added to the glamour of the day.

It was like no horse show Paulo had ever seen. It was a celebration. Paso Fino owners, or merely admirers, were there from all corners of the nation to watch, to participate, just to be able to tell the people at home that they'd been there.

It was the National.

As they neared the show ring a sun-baked woman of perhaps forty stopped in front of them and said, "Excuse me, are you Diego Mendez?"

Diego gave her a nod that was almost a bow.

"How do you do, sir? I'm Martha Scatlin, I'm from Connecticut. I've been admiring your Danza in the barn there, and I was told that you are a breeder, in Puerto Rico, is that right? Then you might be able to help me with a problem I'm having in training a young horse of mine. I understand that you people down there have mastered the technique of—"

Paulo excused himself and left Diego searching for the right words, in English, to explain the importance of head set and balance.

Back in Danza's stall, Paulo once again picked up the horse's front hoof and pressed his thumb against the frog, the horny cushion that bore much of Danza's weight, and which should be almost as insensitive as the hoof itself.

When Paulo pressed, Danza jerked away.

The pain was still there. It had been last night after they'd unloaded Danza and Nibs from the Feldens' trailer; it had been there early this morning when Paulo arrived from the motel.

Marilyn's head appeared over the stall door. "How is he?"

"Still some soreness there when I press on his frog."

"Lead him around once."

Paulo took Danza's halter and led the horse in a circle around the stall. There was no apparent soreness in his step.

"I think he'll be okay," Marilyn said with twelve-year-old authority. "It's a grass ring. Come on, quit worrying about him. They're starting the Weanling classes. Let's go watch."

They found seats in the bleachers that flanked the ring and watched the Weanling Colt class, or went through the motions of watching it. For Paulo there was only Danza, today. Danza, whose acid-damaged feet still hurt under pressure. Danza, who must now take Bonanza's place as herd sire, back home.

Danza, whose return had demanded the sacrifice of his sire.

Danza, who might return to Puerto Rico bearing the prestigious title of American National Grand Champion and by so doing would all but assure the future financial success of Mendez and Camacho, Paso Fino Breeders.

Danza. His friend.

Diego climbed the bleachers and settled with a grunt beside Paulo. His face was more animated than Paulo had ever seen it. *Like a little boy at a carnival,* Paulo thought. He wanted to stretch out his hand and touch Diego, to embrace him, to express in some way the emotions inside him, a churning of feelings that swirled around Diego and Major Kessler, and Bonanza. But he didn't know how.

Instead, he said, "What did that woman want?"

Diego laughed. "Some advice. She said her horse was trotty. I looked at the horse and told her to trim an inch off his heels on his hind feet. She was so impressed she wants to buy horses from us."

Paulo caught his breath. "Will you sell to her?"

"Mmm. I might. She was a nice lady. We've got a flashy little two-year-old colt at home—Sol, remember him? Buckskin? I priced him at two thousand to her. She's flying down next week to see him."

Paulo settled back and digested this. He didn't say, "I thought you said you'd never sell stallions to the States," nor did he say, "That's twice as much as you could get for that colt at home." But he felt a curious easing of pressure, as though a door had been opened.

The interminable morning classes finally passed, the Bella Forma Grand Champion declared and applauded and draped with a huge collar of purple satin, from which hung a mammoth rosette reaching to the horse's knees. An hour lunch break was called, during which Paulo sat rigid in his bleacher seat and looked at his watch every five minutes.

Time to go to Danza. At last.

He found Diego already in the stall, brushing

down Danza's satin flanks with the Feldens' softest dandy brush.

The old man looked over his shoulder at Paulo. "I'll get him ready. You go get dressed."

In the Feldens' trailer Paulo pulled on his random-gathered show suit; Marilyn's hat and Mr. Felden's boots, a dark green bolero suit borrowed from an exhibitor Paulo didn't even know, ruffled white shirt borrowed from someone else. The boots were too big, but Paulo spread his toes and duck-walked back to the stable.

As soon as he had settled into the saddle, Paulo felt a sense of rightness. For a moment he forgot Danza's feet and his own curled toes and the borrowed suit. Danza's power, Danza's excitement came reverberating through the saddle, through the reins.

They waited outside the ring for the completion of the Classic Fino Mares class. Danza snatched at his bit. Standing in place, neck arched, tail lifted in a proud plume, the stallion began lifting his feet in the rhythm of the fino gait. He danced the dance that was in his blood, and in Paulo's.

"Hold him still," Diego growled as he tried to give Paulo's boots a final polish.

"I'm . . ."

Suddenly the major was there, standing close beside Danza's shoulder. His eyes met Paulo's with a look of tentative warmth, as though the man were unsure of his welcome.

"Paulo, Mr. Mendez." The major turned and offered his hand to Diego. "I didn't expect to see you here, sir."

"We didn't expect to see you, either," Diego said with an even look.

The major smiled and regained his look of easy composure. "I couldn't miss the National, even if I didn't have an entry this year. I expect to be here as an exhibitor next year, though, with a good weanling Danza colt." He turned to Paulo, and reached up to offer his hand. "Good luck, son."

Emotion choked Paulo, but there was time for only a brief, hard handclasp. Then the loudspeaker blared.

"Classic Fino Stallions, into the ring, please."

With unflawed cadence Danza moved forward into the emerald oval. The sun shot copper daggers from his coat. His mane lifted in a luxurious froth about Paulo's hands. Other stallions followed them into the ring and around the green-hedged oval, but Paulo was unaware of them.

His whole world condensed into just Danza, just the flutter-flow of Danza's movement over the grass.

It came to him that there was an unusual element of joy in Danza today. It's having me back, Paulo thought. Or else he knows this is the National.

Around and around they went, like a train of twelve cars, bay and black and rich dark chestnut, gray and roan and pinto, palomino and buckskin and cremella. The stallions moved with necks tightly arched, nostrils flared as though they were ready to burst with power and spirit. Yet the twelve riders sat motionless, heads high, backs straight, hands still. They might have been sailing on air, so effortlessly did they glide.

The judge spoke to the steward; the steward faced the

announcer and made a circling motion with his hand.

"Reverse, please," the announcer called.

With no visible break in speed or stride, twelve stallions circled toward the inside of the ring and continued to fino in the opposite direction.

Paulo listened and felt Danza's beat beneath him. No sign of fatigue yet, nothing unusual in the footfalls. No pain yet.

After what seemed to Paulo an inordinate number of laps around the ring with frequent reversals of direction, the announcer requested a lineup. Gratefully Paulo guided Danza to his place at the end of the line of horses standing facing the center of the ring.

He glanced down the line for his first look at the men and women with whom he was competing. Among them were the best of the professionals, the toughest competition in the country. But that's the way it should be, he realized. What good is a National Championship unless it *is* won from among the best? If the professionals were better than he was, then they deserved the win, not him.

Two ring stewards appeared and took their places facing each other about twenty feet apart.

The judge nodded to Paulo, and indicated the stewards. "Figure eight, please," he said.

Paulo halted Danza between the stewards, and tipped his hat to the judge, them moved Danza forward, around the left-hand steward, across the center, around the right. It was a good figure-eight. He could feel it. Good controlled turns, no swinging out of Danza's hindquarters, no double tracking, no break in the rhythm of his gait.

One by one the other eleven stallions came forward and maneuvered through the pattern, some well, some with too much excitement, too little steadiness at the corners.

The judge spoke to the stewards and they stepped closer to one another, shrinking the figure eight by half. Then he motioned to Paulo and to another rider, a woman on a gray who had done an exceptionally smooth job.

The judge approached them. "I'd like you to go through the figure eight together, please, and continue until I call a halt.

They began weaving around the stewards, Danza in the lead, the gray close behind. Neither horse broke. As the circling continued, the horses began to separate so that there were near-collisions at the crossover point. The grueling contest went on. Both horses were lathered. The unmaned side of Danza's neck was rubbed to a white froth by the rein. Sweat ran down his legs, and down Paulo's back beneath the borrowed jacket and the borrowed shirt.

Paulo began to feel the strain in Danza. *It can't go on much longer,* he thought, *or Danza will break. Or the other horse.*

Still the judge watched, impassive.

The gray was ahead of Danza now, circling about four feet out from the steward. On a sudden impulse Paulo gave Danza a light leg-squeeze and they moved up beside the gray, inside the curve of the other horse's track.

A rustle of surprise went through the audience.

Danza was forced to maneuver a turn tighter than he'd ever done before, and he had to do it with no hesitation, no flaw in the rhythm of his steps. Paulo held his breath. He felt his boot brush the steward's arm.

Around the corner! No break. The gray came up on Danza's other side and again they circled the steward in the opposite direction now, but with Danza again on the inside.

Again Danza executed the turn without a flaw.

Applause, cheering, came dimly through the ringing in Paulo's ears as the judge, without the formality of signals to the announcer, motioned the two riders to a halt.

There was barely time to return to the lineup before the announcer caroled, "Winner of the Classic Fino Stallions class, Danza! Owner, Diego Mendez, rider Paul Camacho."

Paulo felt almost too weak to wrap his arm around the trophy handed up to him by a grinning little girl in Spanish dress. Someone fastened the neck ribbon with its huge rosette around Danza's neck and a photographer said, "Smile a little. Your horse looks happier than you do."

*It's just the Stallion class,* Paulo told himself as he rode Danza out of the ring. *Now he has to win the Championship class.*

Away from the ring entrance and the congratulating crowd, surrounded only by Diego and the Feldens, Paulo relaxed, and Danza relaxed.

And then Paulo felt it. Danza's back arched ever so slightly as he sought to bring his hind feet under him, to ease his weight off of his front legs. As he set down each front hoof, he snapped it up again instantly, as though he were walking on fire.

Paulo slipped to the ground. "He's limping," he said quietly to Diego. "All of a sudden, just now. I don't think he was, in the ring."

"Let's get him into his stall."

"The Championship class—" Paulo said. He stopped and looked back toward the ring. Classic Fino Geldings were in the ring, a large class. The Championship class for the top two winners in the Stallion, Mare, and Gelding classes would follow just after this class. Fifteen minutes, maybe. Paulo felt a rising panic. A decision—

By the time they reached the stall, Danza was walking with such an obvious limp that people turned their heads to watch, and stretched their faces in sympathy.

In the privacy of their stall, Diego and Paulo faced each other across Danza's saddle.

"Just all of a sudden," Paulo said helplessly.

Diego looked steadily at the boy. "An athlete blocks out the pain while he's in the game," he said. "The pain comes later."

"We'd better pull him from the Championship class, then?"

Diego said, "That's up to you. If you ask him for more, Danza will give it to you. He'll go till he drops, for you. You know that."

"Yeah, I know," Paulo said quietly. "Will you go tell the officials, Grandfather? I'll take care of Danza."

He began unbuckling the saddle's girth, his head turned away from Diego. A hand lay warmly on his shoulder. For an instant Paulo leaned back into the strength of the old man behind him. Then Diego was gone, and there was unsaddling to do.

# *Fifteen*

A sunset breeze winnowed the grasses of the meadow and turned them golden-green. Far in the distance, a path of red led out across the Caribbean Sea, from the coast to the ball of red that hung at the horizon. Already the forest that rimmed the meadow was green-black with approaching night, but its blackness was shot through with darting birds of brilliant colors.

"Ko-*kee*, Ko-*kee*," the coqui frogs' chorus blanketed the island with their dusk-song.

At the crest of the meadow's highest rise, a sunset-red stallion stood facing into the breeze, his head low, relaxed, his nostrils opening easily to take in old, loved scents. His forelock blew across his eyes and buried his ears in its fullness; his tail snagged on high-growing grass.

A boy, a young man, stood against the horse's shoulder, his arm thrown over the arch of the neck and lost in the wealth of mane that fell on the other side.

There was ease in the lines of the two figures as they supported one another. Peace.

A long journey, completed.

| DATE DUE | BORROWER'S NAME |
|----------|-----------------|
|          |                 |
|          |                 |
|          |                 |
|          |                 |